WHIRLWIND ROMANCE

Visit us at www.boldstrokesbooks.com

By the Author

Jolt

Whirlwind Romance

WHIRLWIND ROMANCE

by
Kris Bryant

2016

ISBN 13: 978-1-62639-581-7

THIS TRADE PAPERBACK ORIGINAL IS PUBLISHED BY
BOLD STROKES BOOKS, INC.
P.O. BOX 249
VALLEY FALLS, NY 12185

FIRST EDITION: FEBRUARY 2016

CREDITS
EDITOR: ASHLEY TILLMAN
PRODUCTION DESIGN: SUSAN RAMUNDO
COVER DESIGN BY SHERI (GRAPHICARTIST2020@HOTMAIL.COM)

Acknowledgments

A special thank you to Radclyffe and Sandy Lowe for taking another chance on me. Being a part of BSB has changed my life and I will always be thankful for the opportunity to tell my stories. My fantastic editor Ashley only makes my stories ten thousand times better, and I am so happy and grateful she's got my back. Thank you to Cathy Frizzell, MJ Williamz, Laydin Michaels, Heather Blackmore, and so many other BSB writers who took me under their wings and showed me the ropes. Thank you to Kathy Creedon for giving me the title when I completely drew a blank. A special shout out to KB Draper and Stacy Wilmes for finding me here in Kansas City and keeping me on task. Their encouraging words make me love them even more. As always, thank you Deb, Patty, Shelly L., all of my friends who realize writing is my true passion, and to my parents and my sister for your love and understanding.

Dedication

To Deb who always gives me the best ideas,
fills my heart, and pushes me to finish what I start.

CHAPTER ONE

I can feel Hunter staring at me, but I ignore her and continue tapping my fingers against the steering wheel, my eyes focused on the swirling dark clouds in the distance. The sweet, wet heaviness of the storm filters into the SUV and I crack the window to catch a deeper breath. We have been waiting for this all day and my pulse quickens as I put the car into gear and swing onto the highway.

"I'm not answering you on purpose," I say. I see her roll her eyes and exhale. "We've got bigger things going on." I point to the dark wall cloud looming in front of us. Mother Nature has been teasing us all morning and we've finally caught a break and moved beside the storm, ready to engage when that wicked whip of a tornado twists from the cloud. I smile. This is what I live for. This is my excitement. Forget closing big corporate deals. Too structured for me. I would poke sharp objects in my eyes if I had to wear a suit to work every day and kiss the asses of Ivy League assholes. I like the unpredictable. I like bantering with Mother Nature.

"At some point we will have to talk about it," Hunter says. She updates Doppler on the laptop, and hooks up the GPS. Somehow, some way, we will get from point A to point B, fields between the storm and us are fair game as long as our faithful Chevy Tahoe will get us there. Central Iowa is a maze of barbed wire, cornfields, and dirt roads. I've been known to push through a gate or two to get the perfect video and data. Somebody has to do it and University of Oklahoma is willing to give me the tools to get out here and get it done. Hunter and I are just a small part of the whole team, but I like to think we are the best. "I'd like to know if I have a job next year or if I have to start sending my resume out to other colleges. Or, God forbid, television news stations." She's sulking and I'm going to let her. We can talk about it later.

"Do you see that?" I point at a large white object, the size of a baseball, bouncing in the street before we drive over it. "There's another one!" The excitement lasts about ten seconds only to be replaced by genuine fear when we realize we are under a barrage of hailstones. Man, this is going to be a whopper. I cringe as they pound the hood and roof and pray the windows stay intact. I have nowhere to go so I slow down and pull onto the shoulder. It's so loud outside that I can barely hear Hunter muttering a mere two feet away. She's hovering over the equipment as if protecting it from hailstones that might smash through the car. I'd smile at her commitment, but I'm too nervous for our safety right now. As much as I would like to open the door and pick a few stones up, I know I'd get about two feet before being bludgeoned to death by one.

Sometimes Mother Nature likes to toy with me. The good news is that most hailstorms don't last very long. I hear whimpering and notice that Maddox, my sweet pit bull, has crawled from the very back and is now tucked behind my seat as low as he can go. Poor baby. I reach behind my seat and pet him, doing my best to soothe both of us. Hunter grabs my camera, ready to take photos of the giant stones as soon as it's safe. I don't even have to tell her, she just knows that we aren't leaving until we get documentation. We really don't have time, but these are the largest we've seen and we will regret it if we don't.

"Look at this. This core is huge," Hunter says. I lean over to see the screen and shriek as a softball size hailstone bounces right on the hood of the car in front of us. Practically in Hunter's lap now, I sheepishly grin at her and crawl back to my seat. She shakes her head. "You're such a girl sometimes." She's never scared of anything. Last season we saw about two dozen tornadoes up close and personal, some of them F2 and F3 on the Fujita scale, and I'm sure her heartbeat never got above sixty beats per minute. Sometimes in this SUV, I feel like a trapped rabbit and when I see scary shit like a tornado in our path, I'm sure my heart is going to burst. I'm glad she's with me. She's my rock.

"It's so weird that hail just quits," I say. Taking my camera from Hunter's hands, I jump out and start snapping photos. Hunter grabs the cooler and starts picking up some of the larger stones in the grass in front of the car.

"This is probably the one that hit the hood right in front of us." She palms a stone that she can barely hold in her hand. It's as large as a softball. I take a few photos of her holding it before she tucks it in the cooler. "We should get going. We're missing a lot of the action." We've only been out of the car two minutes, but in the world of storm chasing, two minutes can seem like a lifetime. I glance over the car as we climb back into it and cringe. Thankfully, the windows aren't cracked, but the hood and doors are beat to hell. Dr. Williams isn't going to be happy. Our insurance is sky high with good reason. Hunter grabs the laptop and studies it before she points us east. "We need to head east if we are going to catch anything. I don't see any rotation yet, but there is a tiny hook forming in this cell southeast of us. If we turn left down Highway 33, we might just cut it off." I hear and feel hailstones crunching under the tires and try my best to maneuver back onto the highway. Most sane people are home. Not us. I tell myself that we are gathering important information about storms and tornadoes and trying to make the world safer, but deep down, I know it's really just for the thrill of the chase.

CHAPTER TWO

So that didn't work out the way we planned. We couldn't intercept the tornado because atmosphere instability and wind shear gave it a different path than we predicted. That happens out here a lot. Science can only get you so far. The rest is up to Mother Nature and luck. It's five in the afternoon and we need gas and energy. I'm sure Maddox needs a break, too. The Mobile Truck Stop is a regular stop for us. I pull up to a gas pump and gingerly step out of the SUV, stretching my body, frowning at the snaps and pops I hear. I'm only twenty-eight, but I sometimes feel like I have the body of an eighty-year-old after being hunched over a steering wheel for eight hours. Hunter jumps out and opens the door for Maddox who wastes no time in running off toward the corn field beside the truck stop.

"Well, he's pretty excited to be free," Hunter says. We smile and watch him as he sniffs and marks every budding plant he sees. After a few minutes, I whistle for him and he bolts back to me, his tongue hanging out. I swear he's smiling. I keep him close because in small towns in the middle of Nowhere, Iowa, if the locals don't recognize your dog, they shoot first, then ask questions. And pit bulls aren't considered cute and cuddly dogs. Maddox wouldn't hurt a flea, but I understand people's hesitation around him. He looks like he's killed a few people in his life. I got him when he was still a puppy, but not before he was wrapped in barbed wire and left for the coyotes in the hills behind the university. His body still shows the scars, but I believe he's forgotten about that and has happily moved on as our traveling mascot. He jumps back into the car and I pump gas while Hunter visits the ladies' room.

"Tris, what in the hell happened to you guys?" I hear yelled from somewhere behind me. I turn to find Adam and Brian headed toward me, their eyes huge, staring at the SUV. I shrug like it was no big deal. Our two teams left OU a few days ago, both of our vehicles smooth and free of blemishes.

"Did you not see the hailstorm a few hours ago?" I ask. I want to reach over and close their mouths because now I'm starting to feel bad. I turn around and stare with them. Yep. It's bad. I remember the cooler and open the door to show them the enemy in the form of ice balls. I smile because they haven't melted much. "Look at this baby." I hold up the large hailstone and they 'oooh' and 'ahhh' collectively.

"That's incredible. I'm surprised you didn't lose any windows." I nod in agreement. I can't imagine being out of commission for days or a week waiting on new glass.

"Hi, guys," Hunter says. She slides back up next to me, her hand digging around in a bag of Fritos. So the crappy eating has begun. "Pretty amazing, huh?"

"Williams is going to shit when he sees the car," Brian says. Secretly I know he's happy that this happened to us, but I don't care. Dr. Williams respects me and my work. This isn't the first time I've been somewhat responsible for destroying school property and I doubt it will be the last. Storm chasing is dangerous and we all know what we are getting into every season. Spring in the Midwest boils up large and wicked thunderstorms that produce vortexes of swirling, destructive cyclonic winds. It's our job to record as much information about them, while trying our best to keep people safe. We record wind speeds, plot paths in relation to the storms, and video what we see. It's not glamorous, but it's fascinating.

"Did you guys get any footage?" I ask.

"We were too far away, but I heard on the CB that some new chasers scored video," Adam says. That piques my interest. I hope it wasn't some college frat boys looking for a cheap thrill. It seems like every time new chasers post videos to the Internet, twenty more teams of amateur photographers hit the road hoping to get lucky, too. Only they end up getting in the way of the professionals or worse, end up getting hurt.

"Probably some stupid kids somewhere," Hunter says. She's more vocal than I am at all of the new chasers every season. Most go away after one or two seasons. We are a tight knit community. With the CBs and only a few truck stops with high-speed internet work stations sprinkled throughout the Midwest, we really get to know one another on the road because we all gravitate to the same places. It's as if we are a traveling convention three months out of the year.

"Are you guys moving on or staying put until morning?" I don't want to ask which direction they are headed. Professional courtesy. There is a front passing the Rockies tomorrow and looks to split in Kansas and head north to Nebraska and south to Oklahoma. Hunter and I decided to head northwest. The front is supposed to stall for a bit around Lincoln and with the unstable spring air, a tornado sighting seems more plausible.

"We are going to drive for a few more hours tonight then call it a day," Brian says. I nod in agreement. I really want a healthy meal, a hot shower, and I want to sprawl out on a big bed, but if we stop now, we might miss the action in the morning.

"We are going to stretch for a bit and then head out, too." I wave good-bye and head into the truck stop. It's one of the nicer ones we've found, with fast internet access, hot showers, and you can even rent a cot for a few hours or overnight. As I head toward the restrooms, I see a man and a woman hunched over a computer in the rustic media center and I almost stumble from stopping too quickly. I sort of recognize the man, but I've never seen the woman before. She's stunning. She has long, straight strawberry blonde hair that she is twisting in her right hand. She is pointing at the screen with her left hand and her pursed mouth splits into a beautiful smile at whatever she is watching. I realize I'm blatantly staring so I pick up my pace and head to the bathroom. I want to make sure I look presentable before I introduce myself to her. Maybe by then I'll remember how I know the guy she is sitting with and it won't be so awkward when I butt into their conversation. I stand at the sink, stare at myself in the mirror, and try to figure out how I can make myself look better with absolutely nothing but a rubber band. I'm not MacGyver. My hair is just long enough to throw up, but leaves me with a short, stubby tail that Hunter grabs from time to time to piss me off. I decide to leave my hair down. It's dark brown, almost black, thanks to my Cherokee heritage. My eyes are dark brown, too, and I have the Native American high cheekbones. I've been called attractive many times, but right now, I'm not seeing it. I see frumpy, wrinkly, exhausted Tristan staring back at me. Maybe today isn't the best day to hit on an attractive woman. I straighten out my clothes the best I can and give myself a last minute look over before I nod confidently and walk out. They are both still sitting there, staring at their computer so I take a moment to concentrate on him. How do I know him?

"Tristan. Hi. It's me, Gage," he says. Gage! I only know one Gage and he works for Oklahoma State, our rivals. Boom. His face matches up with a few functions I attended last year off season including two fundraisers and a job fair. I breathe a sigh of relief. Now engaging them in conversation isn't going to be awkward.

"How are you?" I ask. I'm respectfully maintaining eye contact with him, but my peripheral vision is devouring his partner. I can tell she is staring at me, and even though I know it's to be polite, I'm hoping she feels that little tingle of excitement, too. Without waiting for an introduction, I reach my hand out to her and introduce myself. "Hi, I'm Tristan. Tristan Stark." When we make eye contact, her eyes narrow and her right brow lifts ever so slightly. Up close, she's even more beautiful than I thought. I expect freckles across the bridge of her nose, but her skin is smooth and fair. Her eyes dart all over my face and for a brief moment, I'm actually self-conscious.

"Tris works for OU. She's one of the top meteorologists there. Watch out for her," Gage says.

"Thanks, Gage. It's good to see you again. Are you guys just getting started this season?"

"We've been out for a few days," he says.

"Hi. I'm Kate." She doesn't offer me her last name and that surprises me. She looks me over again. I can't tell if she's interested or just curious. When she finally smiles, I relax. I want to sit down and get to know her, but after she shoots me that beautiful smile, she returns to her laptop and I'm forgotten. She's completely engrossed in a video and suddenly I'm feeling like the third wheel. Awkward.

"Nice to meet you, Kate. Gage, I'll see you two around."

"Sorry, Tristan. We are just in the middle of something here. I'm sure we'll see each other around." I wink at Gage and casually walk out. My tender ego needs some alone time. Hunter is sitting in the SUV, ready to navigate by the time I get back. "I just ran into Gage from State. He's chasing this season and has a new chaser with him. She's pretty, but doesn't seem very personable."

"Your charms didn't work on her?" Hunter asks. She looks incredulously at me and I playfully smack her on her arm. We both know how clumsy I am around beautiful women. Usually, I clunk along until I get it right, but Kate quickly checked me out, then completely blew me off like I was nobody. Ouch.

"Maybe she's Gage's girlfriend," Hunter says. Hmm. I guess I didn't even think that she might be straight. "Not every beautiful woman is gay. Look at me. I'm sure you thought I was gay when you first met me." This is true. Hunter is just shy of six feet tall. Her hair is cut short in the back with long sweeping bangs in the front that she constantly swipes out of her eyes. She has about ten piercings, wears no makeup, and has been with her boyfriend James for two years now.

"Wishful thinking," I say. She playfully bats her eyelashes at me. I roll my eyes back at her. "Let's get out of here so we hit Omaha before dark." It's almost five thirty now so we should hit town by eight. I give Maddox a piece of jerky, which he happily chomps on and we hit the road again.

CHAPTER THREE

A re you guys following us?" Gage asks. I almost roll my eyes at him, but stop when I see Kate. She's pale and beautiful and I can't stop staring at her. She looks even better now than she did earlier in the day when we first met.

"You saw the same thing on the radar that we did, huh?" Hunter asks. She shakes Gage's hand and introduces herself to Kate. This time, Kate is polite and gives Hunter her undivided attention and her full name, Kate Brighten. I want to pout. She couldn't have cared less when Gage introduced us earlier. When she turns to me, she smiles and stares for a few seconds longer than socially acceptable and, suddenly, I've forgiven her for practically ignoring me earlier.

"It's kind of late for dinner, but do you want to join us?" he asks.

"Sure," I say. Hunter smiles sweetly at me and I know I'm going to pay for it later. Our plan was to grab a quick bite at the restaurant within walking distance of the motel and head back and crash. Instead, we are seated at a round table in a dark restaurant that smells like wood panel and stale potpourri. I'm glad that we got our room first and had a chance to freshen up. I'm in clean clothes and feel human again. We sit down and order beers before looking at the menu. I'm pretty sure I know the menu without even looking at it from the smells coming from the kitchen. Meatloaf, fried chicken, burgers, fries, and nothing really healthy.

"How long have you guys been chasing?" Kate asks. Before I have a chance to answer, Hunter pipes up.

"Well, for this season, we just headed out a few days ago, but we've been chasing for six seasons now."

Kate looks pleasantly surprised. "You've probably seen a ton of tornadoes then, huh?"

I nod ready to tell tales of our adventures and mishaps when Gage interrupts.

"Kate got a real treat today. We caught that tornado near Cedar Rapids. The video is stunning," he says. He's not bragging. Gage is sweet.

"We heard some new chasers got it. Congrats," Hunter says. She's so diplomatic. Again, I want to pout. I haven't had a chance to talk and nobody seems to care.

"They are saying it was an F2." He refers to the Fujita scale, the scale meteorologists use to rate a tornado's intensity based on wind speed and destruction. "I'm so glad I'm finally out in the storms. It gets boring working in the lab all day, every day. Seeing a tornado up close was fantastic. More than what I expected."

"I agree. It was amazing. It's one thing to watch videos, see photos, and study radar of tornadoes, but a completely different experience seeing one in person," Kate says. She's leaning forward in her chair, her right hand gripping her beer tightly. Her enthusiasm is endearing. She turns her attention to me and gives me an award winning smile. I'm pretty sure my heart skips a few beats. "You're so lucky to have done this so many times already."

"It never gets old. Are you a student at OSU or on the staff there?" I ask. Her smile drops immediately, but she covers up quickly and answers.

"I'm working on my Masters degree." That's all she gives me. She's driving me crazy. One minute, she's up and happy and I feel like I'm floating, the next she's down and I feel like I'm giving an interview.

"Is your undergrad in meteorology or something else?" I ask, trying to engage her further.

"Yes. I've always been fascinated with weather," she says. "Oklahoma is probably one of the best places to be if you want to study it."

"OSU is a good school, but OU is better." I wink so everybody knows I'm kidding. Gage laughs. Kate doesn't look amused. As a matter of fact, the more we talk, the quieter she gets. I must have struck a nerve when I asked her about school for some reason. I decide to just keep my mouth shut. I order another beer and lean back and sulk the best I can without looking like I've checked out of the conversation. Thank God Hunter is amusing them with stories.

Our food arrives and we dig in. I didn't realize I was so hungry. Three of us ordered burgers and fries, but Kate opted for a somewhat healthy salad she convinced them to dig up. I feel guilty. Of course, she's probably a size two from the looks of it, and on a good day I fit into a size six. I add more ketchup to my fries.

"Are you guys together?" Kate asks. I've just taken a huge bite out of my burger and my only response is a snort. Hunter grins.

"Ah, no. We're best friends. I have a boyfriend and Tris has a fear of commitment," she says. I shoot her an evil look. "Well, not a fear really. She's just waiting for Ms. Right." And there it is. Hunter doesn't care who knows I'm a lesbian. I tend to be a little more discreet. "Are you and Gage together?" Kate and Gage both shake their heads no. Gage tells us about his girlfriend back in Stillwater, Oklahoma and how they are planning on getting married and starting a family soon. I'm officially bored.

I want to know about Kate. I want to know why she gave me a strange look when Hunter said I was looking for Ms. Right. I want to know if she's intrigued or even interested. I find she's not making eye contact with me and my heart sinks a little. I order another beer and Hunter nudges me. I look at my watch. It's barely ten at night. We have plenty of time to sleep it off.

"Hunter's boyfriend is great. He's in a band and plays a lot in Oklahoma. He even plays down at OSU. You guys should check him out sometime. If you are into rock music," I say.

"I'm more into country, but next time he's down, I'll be sure to tell the others about him," Gage says.

"What kind of music do you like, Kate?" I ask. I'm determined to get her to open up more. I can't tell if she's shy or just uninterested.

"I like it all really. Maybe not country so there's always a fight in the car on what we should listen to," she says. Gage smiles at her. I get the feeling he gets his way most of the time. As nice as he is, he seems to be old school where men are always right and women are just there to look pretty.

"We have a rule in our SUV. Whoever is driving, gets to pick the music. Thankfully, we like the same stuff," Hunter says. "There isn't much to do except listen to music or audio books or talk when you are in the car for months at a time."

Kate looks surprised. "How long do you chase?"

"The whole season. Until the end of June usually," I say.

"I'm only out for a few weeks this time," Kate says. "Once I'm done, another person in our study group will head out with Gage. And then another." It surprises me that they don't have more chasers out with all of their funding and equipment. Based on the Frankenstein looking vehicle out in the parking lot, their school has plenty of money to spend on chasing.

"Well, here's to a great tornado season," Gage says. He tips his beer and we all clink longnecks. I can feel Kate finally look at me and I turn to meet her gaze. This time she doesn't turn. I take a long drink and keep staring until she finally looks away.

❖

"Did I really reach out and touch her hair?" I ask. Hunter loops her arm with mine as we walk back to the motel. She laughs and kisses the top of my head.

"No, but the way you were looking at her was making me uncomfortable. Like you wanted to touch her hair and other things on her body." I cringe. I have zero coolness. I've never been suave, especially with the ladies. Throw alcohol into the mix and forget it.

"I wonder if she noticed," I say. Hunter squeezes my arm to let me know and I groan. "I'm a total idiot. Don't let me drink so much next time, okay?" She opens the motel door and lets Maddox out before she tucks me into bed. He returns, jumps on the bed, and burrows next to me. I sigh happily. Who needs a woman when you've got a warm, snuggly dog to keep you company?

Hunter gets into her bed. "Are we ever going to talk about the grant?"

I forgot she asked me earlier in the day. I roll over to face her.

"I haven't heard yet. That's why I haven't wanted to talk about it. Dr. Williams hasn't said anything and I'm going with no news is good news." I start cracking my knuckles. I'm worried.

"Don't we usually hear something by now?" Hunter asks. She's right. We start the season off knowing how much we have in the budget for the next season. I plan on storm chasing for the university as long as we're funded. "You at least teach classes in the fall. I have to know what happens to me by the summer."

"I know. I'll send Williams an e-mail in the morning. Right now I don't think I can type on this stupid phone." Call me old fashioned, but I need a computer with a decent size monitor in order to send or read any correspondence. I don't understand how people run businesses with a two inch by four inch screen.

"Okay. Get some sleep. We'll worry about it later," Hunter says. Her breathing evens out and I'm jealous at how quickly she falls asleep.

❖

I'm in complete denial that it's morning. Hunter is bouncing on the bed. Little does she know that I'm about thirty seconds from throwing up on her.

"Get off of me." I try to bury myself deeper into the covers. "It can't possibly be time to get up."

"Not only is it time, but I've been following the path of the storm and we aren't that far away. Maybe an hour. If we leave in twenty minutes, we have time to find the perfect spot and maybe catch a tornado." She rips back the covers and I growl in frustration. I sprawl out and flip her off. "Get dressed." I don't care that I'm barely wearing anything. That will teach her to take my covers away.

"I don't feel good," I say. Her grin tells me she knows this and couldn't care less.

"I told you to stop after three beers." She's almost singing it to me. "Go take a quick shower and meet me outside. I've put clothes out for you to wear."

"Who are you, my mother?"

She responds by throwing a pillow that knocks me back down. I want to wallow in self-pity, but I know she's right and the lure of a tornado gets me moving. My shower is thankfully hot and I feel myself slowly waking up. It takes me a few extra minutes to get dressed, but by the time I leave the motel room, I'm able to function normally. Maddox and Hunter are already in the car.

Movement catches my eye across the parking lot and I see Gage and Kate getting into their souped-up truck. I was pretty excited about the metal and Plexiglas box screwed on top of our Tahoe to protect a video camera that we remotely control inside the cab. Their truck makes our SUV look like a Tinker Toy.

I'm surprised when Gage and Kate wave at me. I wave back trying hard not to cringe again remembering last night.

"I'm driving until you start feeling human again," Hunter says. That's fine. I feel like letting somebody else take control. "I picked up biscuits and milk for breakfast. That should help you feel a little better." I nod thanks and start eating. I know the sooner I get something in my stomach, the quicker I'll feel human again. I feed Maddox a biscuit, which he happily munches on.

"So tell me exactly what I said to Kate," I say. I remember trying to be a little flirty. Touching her arm, laughing at what she said. I groan just remembering bits and pieces.

"You really weren't that bad, I promise," Hunter says. "You were just very excited that she was there, that's all. You were sweet. It was cute." That's a sure sign I said idiotic things. I sigh heavily and Hunter punches my arm. This day can only get better.

CHAPTER FOUR

Most people relax on the weekend. Mother Nature doesn't care so we are on call twenty-four seven. It's Sunday afternoon and we have been busting our asses every single day since we hit the road over a week ago. Right now, it looks as if we are in the middle of something awful. Doppler is a swirl of dangerous red and dark orange and I can tell Hunter is starting to get nervous. It's raining and dark. I have my eyes glued to the sky. Hunter is ten and two at the wheel, her keen eyes focused ahead.

"I've got a bad feeling about this," she says. I nod, still looking at the sky. Somehow we have managed to squeeze the car in between two wall clouds that could drop twisters at any moment. For the first time, I hope I'm wrong. If we get flanked by tornadoes, the best we can hope for is that they don't merge and swallow us whole. Merging tornadoes is rare, but knowing our luck today, it will probably happen. Maddox is getting restless so I know shit is about to go down.

"There." I point the video camera to the left to capture the event. I call it in on the CB and dial the local news station. I use hands free and let Hunter speak because I'm trying to get photos from inside the car. We are trying to gather pressure readings and temperature shifts of tornadoes, but photos and videos are just as important. The wind is fierce and the car is getting rocked around. Hunter gives them our location and, while we are still on the phone, Hunter points to the right of us. Son of a bitch. Another twister. She calmly reports that one as well, mentioning the names of the gravel roads we are zipping past so that people in the storm's path head to safety right away. We have twisters on both sides of us and a wicked storm pushing us forward. Hunter hangs up, steps on the gas, probably hoping to get ahead of them. I don't know what I should be doing besides pray. I'm actually shaking. The video camera on top of the Tahoe is recording the left tornado, so I remotely turn it to video the right one, too. I don't think we're going to outrun this storm.

"Hunter, we are going to have to find a safe place," I say. Her hands leave the wheel for a moment as she holds them up in a surrender to indicate that we are in the middle of nowhere and that really isn't an option. I know this, but I feel like one of us has to at least voice reason even if we don't really believe it. There are gravel roads to our left and right, but shouldn't chance changing directions. Plus, with the speed of this storm, we would get caught if we tried driving on a gravel road, or worse, wreck. Right now, lefty tornado and righty tornado are headed in the same direction as us.

"This is incredible." I don't know how else to explain how I'm feeling and what I'm seeing.

After several minutes of not-so-quietly panicking, we are able to put a little bit of distance between us and the tornadoes. The speedometer is rocking out at eighty five and Hunter shows no signs of slowing down. I'm glad she's driving. "If you slow down a bit, I might be able to get clear video if I lean out the window." I turn to watch out the back of the SUV. "Oh, Hunter, stop! Righty Tornado is turning left and is crossing the road behind us. I want to get this." She slows down and pulls off of the road. I jump out, almost choking myself on my seat belt, and video both tornadoes. They aren't massive at this point, but clearly destructive, if the chunks of metal and pieces of wood thickening the tornado shafts are any indication. After gathering enough video and feeling miserable because I'm now soaked to the bone, I hop back in the car and Hunter squeals back out onto the road.

"That was a little too close for comfort. Check Doppler," she says. I check and see the rotating mass heading northeast.

"I bet they merge. Oh, God, Hunter, if they merge that could be bad." That rarely happens. There aren't many recorded instances of merging tornadoes. "I hope people are safe and in their basements." Once we know the storm is to our left and we're a safe enough distance away, Hunter finds a county road and heads north to intercept it again.

"Let's find out if the tornadoes merged," she says. Her thirst for adventure is insatiable. I want a hot bath, a cold beer, and a soft bed right now. I'm exhausted and I'm not even the one driving.

"I don't know how you do it."

"Do what?" she asks.

"We almost got our asses kicked and you want to go back for more? I'm completely spent. I want to curl up in a ball and go to sleep."

"Can you honestly say you don't want to see if they join? This is the shit we talk about all of the time. We'll keep a safe distance. Keep your eye on Doppler. We can head north, then east and see if they come close. They might just go back up."

She's right. I want to know. We've been doing this a long time and it would be a shame to just tuck our tails and run. "Okay, but at the first sign of trouble, we turn."

The rest of the afternoon is spent chasing the storm, but we never see both tornadoes at the same time again. After thirty miles, we give up. It eventually dies down and Doppler only shows green. We all need a break and dinner. Hunter gets out with Maddox and instructs me to find the nearest, cleanest hotel or motel. It is about thirty minutes away and I take over driving. This is probably the longest half hour drive of the season. We pull up to a rather quaint L shaped hotel and I ask for the room on the corner. It's available. It's easier to sneak Maddox in when we are far away from the office. Not all motels are pet friendly. He's had to stay out in the car before, but tonight we all could use a soft bed. Hunter grabs our bags and we shuffle like zombies into the room. I have the handheld video camera and the laptop, but I'm too tired to do anything. I almost don't want to eat, but I know we have to. Hunter finds a pizza joint and orders a fully loaded pan pizza. I'm asleep before she hangs up. I don't even hear the door when the delivery guy knocks on it. Hunter gently shakes me awake.

"Eat this." She hands me a paper plate with a greasy piece of pizza on it. Maddox leans over me to graciously take Hunter's offering, but I put my hand up between his mouth and the delicious smelling slice.

"That's mine, boy. You can have my crusts."

"I already fed him his food."

We learned a long time ago, the hard way, to not feed him greasy food. It makes for a very uncomfortable and unpredictable car ride the next day. He looks at me guiltily, his sad brown eyes bouncing back and forth between me and the pizza. I tear off the crust before I'm done and feed it to him.

"You know how to play me, Maddox." He licks my face. I'm sure the crumbs he finds are a bonus.

"Can I just say how incredible today was?" Where in the hell does she get her energy? I'm trying to figure out how to take a sip of Coke without actually sitting up in bed and she's pacing the floor in front of me. "How many tornadoes did we see total today? Like four, right? That's crazy. I can't wait to watch the video." I can't wait to go back to sleep. "I wonder if anybody else got video? You should jump online and check." That gives me an idea. I can make casual inquiries about Kate to the group. Maybe I can get more information about her. I reach out for my laptop and fire it up, logging into our community website. It's littered with our colleagues' posts of seeing today's tornadoes. Some have even uploaded their videos already and I'm anxious to show Hunter some of them.

"Oh, look. Here's the video from Cedar Rapids. Gage must have uploaded it." Hunter plops down next to me. We laugh because we can tell it's his first time filming one. I have to look away for a moment because it's so shaky and I'm starting to get nauseous. Hunter and I always use a tripod or monopod for this very reason. Seeing a tornado in person is terrifying and beautiful and it's hard to keep a steady hand with winds and destruction so close. Eventually you learn tricks on how to keep your balance. Criticism aside, it's a wonderful tornado.

"Listen to how stupid excited they are," Hunter says. I can't help but smile when I hear Kate's animated voice. Even thrilled, her voice is raspy and sexy. I wish I would have been able to engage her more in conversation.

"Maybe we should give them a few pointers on how to shoot," I say.

"Definitely. You know it's just a matter of time before everybody else out there gives them crap about it." I find Gage's user name and send him a quick note congratulating him on getting the video, then mentioning a tripod. To my surprise, he instant messages me almost immediately.

Yeah. Some of the guys have already teased me about it.

Well, be proud because you are the only one who got it.

We chat for a little bit longer and I'm tempted to ask about Kate, but I decide to message a few other people who might know her and would be more discreet. I know one of the top dogs in the Meteorology department at OSU so I shoot Clive Lawrence an e-mail about their new team. I ask about Kate in a very vague, roundabout way. Even if he calls me on it, I know he will keep our conversation to himself. Before I'm done reviewing some of the tornado footage from today, I get a response back from Clive.

Tristan,

So are you ever going to work for us here at OSU? Ha. Yes, our department decided to send out more chasers to give our meteorology students the opportunity to see what it's like out there. We picked six of our top students to participate. Kate Brighten is very smart, but keeps to herself. She doesn't talk a lot unless it's about weather. I think she has a younger brother who attends OSU, but don't hold me to it. If you get a chance to pick her brain, do it. Her ideas and theories are exceptional and that's why she's our number one. I hope we can talk her into staying after graduation.

Clive continues on about chasing this season, but I'm re-reading the part about Kate. I'm glad she's not just quiet around me. I wish he would have given more information, but I squirrel away what he's given me. The rest is up to me to gather.

CHAPTER FIVE

We're headed down to the much appreciated continental breakfast when we notice Gage and Kate are checking out of the hotel very early. Gage is shaking and his face is void of all natural color.

"What's going on?" Hunter asks.

"We have to get back to Stillwater. Angie was in a car wreck late last night," Gage says. I dig around in my memory and realize Angie is his girlfriend.

"Oh, no. Is she all right?" I ask. Judging from his appearance, I'm guessing no.

"She's in Intensive Care so I need to get back home," he says. He runs his hand through his already unkempt hair. "Some guy ran a red light and T-boned the car. Thankfully, it was the passenger side and nobody else was in the car, but it still bounced her around pretty hard."

"Good luck and let us know how she's doing," Hunter says.

"Thanks. I will," Gage says.

I can't believe it's not quite seven in the morning and Kate looks stunning. Her hair is pulled back in a long braid and I'm almost certain she doesn't have an ounce of makeup on. She is wearing a fitted T-shirt and khaki pants, the first practical storm chasing outfit I've seen her in. And now she has to turn around and go home for who knows how long.

"I have an idea," I say. Everybody stops and looks at me. I guess I said that out loud.

"Since this is Kate's first season, she's more than welcome to chase with us until you are able to head back out again, Gage. We could meet up somewhere when you are back in action." My palms are sweating. I hope everybody takes it as a goodwill gesture and not some sinister plot to get Kate alone in a car in the middle of nowhere. I push that lustful thought back and put on my serious educator face. "She would be responsible for her own hotel room and food. Trust me, you don't want to be in a room with the three of us." I finally turn my attention to Kate. She stares at me for a full ten seconds before saying anything. I realize I'm holding my breath. I exhale and listen.

"If you and Hunter don't mind. I think that's a great idea."

I manage not to look at Hunter or grin, which is a major feat.

"That's a great idea. More eyes to the skies," Hunter says. Phew. She's not upset. "Since you've already checked out, we can either put your bag in our room or out in the car."

"Wow. Thanks, you guys. That's a really nice offer," Gage says. He helps Kate sort out her luggage from his.

"Do keep us posted on Angie," I say. Gage surprises me by hugging us all before he quickly leaves the lobby.

"Did he just get the call?" Hunter asks.

"No, he missed the call early in the morning and heard the voice mail when he woke up. He called me and we were down here in ten minutes," Kate says. So she really does look this good in the morning.

"I hope she's okay," I say. I'm excited about being close to Kate for at least a few days, but the circumstances are terrible.

"We were on our way to breakfast. Have you eaten yet?" Hunter asks Kate.

"Food sounds great," she says. We grab an open table, set our stuff down, and head for the buffet. I remind myself to not be gluttonous and try to eat somewhat healthily. It's hard when you really want to face dive the scrambled eggs and bacon. I grab a plain waffle, some fruit, and a yogurt. I'm jealous of Hunter's food. She has all the good stuff piled high. She lifts her eyebrow at me and smiles. I frown at her and she hip bumps me. I made the right choice because Kate has almost the exact same thing on her plate.

"So tell us about yourself, Kate," Hunter says as she sits down. I notice Kate stiffen at the question.

"Not much to tell. I'm twenty-four years old, single, and working on my master's degree at OSU." That's all she gives us.

"What do you like to do when you aren't nose deep in textbooks? Do you have any hobbies? Do you have any pets?" I ask. I'm hoping she'll open up more. If she doesn't, it's going to be a very uncomfortable week or however long she is with us.

"I like to water ski, snow ski. I read a lot," she says. That perks my interest.

"What do you like to read?"

"Usually autobiographies, and every so often, I read fiction," she says. Not impressive. I couldn't think of anything more boring to read. I read to escape. I can barely keep up with my own life, let alone read about somebody else's. Smutty romance novels work for me. Especially long hours when I'm the passenger out on the road. I will pick up a historical book, but it has to be about an era, not about one specific person.

"Well, if you feel like branching out, we have a ton of audio books we can listen to," I say. Hunter laughs. She likes it quiet. An audio book is quiet compared to me. They put me to sleep. Great. That's probably been her plan all along.

CHAPTER SIX

So, Hunter, is your boyfriend good with all the time you're apart during the storm season?" Kate asks. This is our second day together and Kate seems to be warming up to us. Hunter is driving so I have the freedom to look around. I like watching Kate when she isn't paying attention. She's always observing and writing things in her notebook. I wonder if she's writing about the weather or creating poetry or sketching cats. I just don't know where to start with her. She has to know I'm interested. According to Hunter, I practically threw myself at her during our dinner a few weeks ago. Was she offended? Excited? She's in the car with us now so either she thinks I'm harmless or she's just used to all of the attention. She's beautiful. The more I'm around her, the closer I want to get.

"Well, he's the drummer in a band and he tours a lot so he doesn't mind when I hit the road." Despite the stereotype, Hunter's boyfriend is perfect for her. Very much a gentleman and loves her dearly. I'm just waiting for her to show up with a big, fat diamond ring on her left hand one day. "It just works. After being cooped up with him all winter, I'm ready for time apart."

"Oh, stop. You two are so cute, it's ridiculous," I say. She smiles at me. Hunter tries to act tough, but she's a softie when it comes to him.

"Tris, what's your story? Why haven't you found Ms. Right?" she asks. She obviously remembers Hunter's reference from our dinner the other night. I want to close my eyes and disappear because that's a hard question.

"Well, maybe I'm just not long term relationship material." I shrug like it's no big deal, but it hurts sometimes. I long for the closeness of a partner. I do miss the touching and the sharing and simple things like good morning kisses and sweet words of encouragement that only a lover can say. How do I convey that without sounding desperate? "It's tough being away from your partner for months at a time, especially during the spring when you're done with the cold weather and want to go out and have fun again. I just haven't connected with any woman yet. Plus, most women glaze over when you start talking about the science of weather, or how exciting it can be when the barometric pressure changes, or when two fronts collide."

"Maybe you aren't meeting the right women," Kate says. "There are a lot of smart, educated women who do care about science and math and who aren't intimidated by another intelligent woman." Christ, she's diplomatic.

"What about you? Are you seeing somebody special?" I ask. I turn the tables and I know it's not nice, but I can't help myself. I have to strike at the opening she created in our conversation.

"No, nobody special. I've really been putting a lot of energy in school and getting the funds to complete my Masters degree. It takes just as much time and effort to do that as it takes to actually get the degree."

"Speaking of which, Tris, have you heard anything back from Williams?" Hunter asks. "Sorry, Kate. We've just been waiting to hear back about a grant and we're starting to get nervous because if we don't get it, we don't do this next year. Tris is lucky, she teaches classes in the fall. But I need to find something else if we didn't get it."

Kate looks at me in surprise.

"I'm not a Neanderthal, you know," I say. She laughs and touches my shoulder. Her fingers are warm and soft and I almost frown when she leans back in the seat, her touch suddenly gone.

"I know. I'm sorry I seem so surprised. You're just super relaxed out here and I'm trying to picture you teaching."

"I do clean up well. I even know how to walk in heels." I put my feet on the dashboard to show off my extremely practical steel toe Red Wing boots. "These are not a fashion statement. These are almost a necessity when chasing." I know I should be offended on some level, but I'm not. I'm just happy she has taken notice of me at all.

"No, no, no. Don't take it like that. You're very calm and it's just refreshing to be around you, both of you. My only other experience with a storm chaser is Gage and he is very anxious and excited," she says.

"Tristan is actually the smartest person I know," Hunter says. Now the conversation becomes uncomfortable. I don't like compliments.

"Stop. I'm not. You're just as smart. Plus, you work with tons of smarties just in our department alone," I say. I'm trying to deflect. I know Hunter thinks she's helping me by building me up, but right now I'm finding it very annoying. I want to impress Kate on my own.

"Well, you're smarter than any of them and you're tons of fun. Besides, you get me and nobody else does," Hunter says.

"Thanks." I avoid Kate's gaze in the mirror on purpose. I want this conversation to turn back to her. I want to know more about why she's single and what she's looking for.

"Kate, have you ever had a serious relationship?" I ask.

"Well, my last relationship was about a year long. I just don't have the time for anything serious right now. I work, I go to school, I go home and sleep. I don't even have time for a pet.

And I would love a pup like Maddox or even a few kitties." Very vague. Perhaps I need a different approach.

"The last woman I dated worked in the math department. She's very smart, but we didn't have a lot in common. She didn't know how to laugh or have a good time," I say.

Hunter laughs. "C'mon, Tris. She was horrible. She was what? Thirty-five going on eighty? And we won't even talk about Julie." I look at Hunter, surprised she would bring up her name, especially in front of somebody I'm interested in.

"So you like older women?" Kate asks, thankfully not wanting more of an explanation about Julie. Maybe she didn't hear Hunter.

"I seem to have more in common with women who are older." I try to be careful with my words, but it sounds bad no matter what. I decide to elaborate. "I haven't really met anybody younger. It's against school policy to date our students even though a few of them are pretty cute." I try humor, but that doesn't seem to work. Hunter comes to my rescue.

"Tris is one of the youngest teachers at the school. She's right. It's hard for her to meet women her age. The choices are gay bars, both of them in town, and online dating. Who wants to do that?" Hunter says.

"Then why are you here in the Midwest?" Kate says. "I mean, isn't most of the action on the East or West Coast?" And there you have it. She's straight. Why else would she say that if she wasn't batting for the other team? Suddenly, I don't want to talk about this anymore.

"I've lived in the Midwest my whole life. My family and my friends are all in Oklahoma. Where are you from?"

"We moved around a lot, but ended up in Oklahoma when I was in high school," she says.

"Where did you live before?" I ask.

"Ladies, I don't mean to interrupt, but we have some questionable clouds around us. Can somebody please check Doppler and tell me what's going on?" Hunter asks. Shitty timing. I refresh the laptop and study the yellow and red on the screen.

"It looks like there is something brewing," I say. Kate is looking at Doppler as well. "Does that look like a wall cloud?" I point to the cloud to our right and we all look. The gray cloud is lowering. It isn't rotating, but we all keep our eyes on it.

"How far out is the rain?" Hunter asks.

"Maybe fifteen minutes or so. Plenty of time to set up in case that drops," I say. Hunter pulls over and we get out of the car. She has the video camera on a tripod and Kate and I have handheld cameras. Nobody is talking and I smile. Silence might just be a superstition for a chaser. We all hold our breath and quietly pray. I sneak a peek at Kate. She looks so serious. Even though she is young, she has an old soul. I work with a lot of young people, but Kate is different. I feel like she's been through something serious in her life already. Maybe she was hurt by somebody. My mind is always thinking of other people's stories, good and bad.

She's wearing jeans and a tight button down shirt with her sleeves rolled to her elbows. She looks beautiful. Her hair is blowing loose from her hair tie and she constantly shakes her head to keep it from getting in her face. She turns to me and for just a few moments, we stare at each other. I'm sure the look I'm giving her is raw with need. I can't tell if she recognizes the look, but she doesn't look away. She slowly smiles at me. My heart beats faster.

"There it is," Hunter says.

"Call it in, call it in," I yell to Hunter, but she's already on the radio and her phone. We've been around long enough to know who to call in each region. Emergency personnel on the

CB and the local news station on the phone. Hunter is better at dealing with crises and disasters than I am. When the traffic clears, Kate and I cross the road to be closer to the tornado. It's moving away from us, dancing slowly across the field. It truly is an amazing act of nature. Seeing one never gets old.

It's hard to see one hit cities and towns. I always cringe when I see a barn or house full of someone's memories explode in its path. I hope that people and animals are safe and always say a little prayer. Growing up, we were always around tornadoes. My father even had a cement bunker down in the basement underneath the front stoop.

I watch Kate marvel at it, snapping a ton of pictures, seemingly torn between watching it and recording it. It's so loud around us that talking is pointless. I'm careful to make sure we don't get too far away from the car. Tornadoes have been known to suddenly switch directions and even though this rope like twister seems lazy, I'm still wary of it. Kate is mesmerized and continues to follow it. I hear Hunter whistle and wave for us. Kate won't be able to hear me so I grab her waist. She tenses up, but I ignore it and pull us closer together so I can yell in her ear.

"Hunter wants to follow it. Let's go."

She turns to me. Our lips are about five inches apart. My legs are almost straddling her thigh because I am so close. I take a step back, giving her space. Her eyes drop to my lips, then back up to my eyes. Her pupils are dilated and her lips are slightly parted. I'm struck with the urge to lean forward and kiss her. I know that her adrenaline rush is because of the tornado, but I want it to be because my nearness affects her. We stare at each other for several moments until I reluctantly point behind us because I know Hunter is anxious to follow the tornado.

Hunter whistles again and the spell is broken. We hurry back to her.

"Let's see where she goes. If this tornado becomes rain wrapped, it's going to be harder to see and that's not good for anybody," Hunter shouts.

We climb in the SUV and Hunter takes off. We drive behind it, giving it space to move freely. Within a few minutes, the twister jumps up and disappears from sight.

"That was quick, but it sure was amazing," Kate says. She's leaning close to us and I can smell her hair. It's a sweet almond scent and I bite my tongue before I accidentally moan with pleasure. I'm an olfactory person. Smells turn me on and Kate is delectable.

"Hopefully, you will get to see a few more with us," Hunter says. We leave the storm and check the computer, trying to track down the next one. I think we both want to impress Kate. Hunter because of scientific reasons, me for personal ones.

CHAPTER SEVEN

Today is one of those days where absolutely nothing is going to happen weather-wise within six hundred miles. We're having a picnic in a small town in rural Kansas. The park is very quaint and old fashioned, but desolate. School is still in session so kids aren't around. I let Maddox run off of the leash, but he stays close by. I think it's because Hunter is feeding him scraps, but she swears she's not. I'd accuse Kate, but she is writing in her book, seemingly ignoring us. We've been with her for four days and I still know virtually nothing about her. It's time to drag information out of her.

"What are you writing?" I ask.

Kate looks at me guiltily and shakes her head. "Nothing important. Just stuff," she says.

I really wish she would open up to us. Not only is she lovely, but extremely mysterious. Even though most people love that quiet and secretive side, I don't. I like talking. I want to get to know her better. I feel like I'm chasing her though. She resumes writing in her notebook and I walk over to Hunter.

"I don't know what else to do," I say. My voice is low so that only Hunter can hear. "I really think she doesn't like me. She blows me off, and every time I try to start a conversation, she is so not interested." Hunter throws a grape at me.

"Quit feeling sorry for yourself. Maybe you're too easy. Or maybe you just annoy her with your incessant talking. You do talk a lot," she says. I know she's kidding, but there is truth to her words. I look back at Kate briefly. Whatever she is writing is personal and seems to be making her sad. She's starting to depress me and that's hard to do. I head for the playground. When life or a beautiful woman brings you down, find the happy place. Right now, that happens to be in the form of a chain link swing with a cracked plastic seat. Maddox follows. I don't want to brood. We don't get days where we can just relax so I try hard to cheer up. Maddox lies in the grass by the swings and I sit there, my face tilted up to the sun enjoying the warmth of the day.

"Want some company?" I hear Kate ask me as she sits in the swing beside me. This is the first time we've been alone.

"Sure. Maybe later we can teeter-totter. I can't do that by myself."

She smiles at my joke. At least I got that from her.

"There is something so peaceful about swinging. We weren't allowed to go to playgrounds when I was growing up," she says.

"Why not?" I can't imagine a child not being allowed on playgrounds.

"My father always thought they were dirty and unsafe," she says.

"Well, that's probably true, but they are a rite of passage." I remember the blisters and calluses on my hands from metal monkey bars and scraped knees from rough terrain. I loved every moment. They don't make playgrounds like that anymore. "And childhood scars make the best stories."

"It wasn't proper for us to associate with kids at the playground," she says. I remember what Hunter just told me, so I try my hardest not to pump her for more information. "And I don't have any scars. Well, ones you can see." Her smile is sad, so I don't press her.

"How many brothers and sisters do you have?" I ask. That's probably a safe question.

"I have a younger brother and a younger sister."

"Are you close to them?" I ask. The chain rustles as she clutches it tighter so I know I'm pushing my luck. I continue as if discussing family isn't a big deal for me. "I have an older brother who torments me any chance he gets, but we're very close. Always have been."

"We used to be close, but things changed," she says. She doesn't elaborate immediately and I don't ask. As hard as it is for me, I decide she'll talk to me when she is ready. "My brother is a freshman at OSU so we do hang out from time to time. But he's busy with football and frat life and I'm busy with school."

"Well, they're missing out on a great sister."

She smiles at me. We swing in companionable silence. Hunter walks over to us and plops on the grass next to Maddox, using his shoulder as a pillow.

"This is a perfect day," Hunter says. "I wish all days were like this."

"No, you don't. You love the thrill of the chase too much," I say.

"Yeah, I do. Well, how about days like this once a week where we only veg out at parks."

"If I was back in Oklahoma, I would grab a book and head out to a park just like this and spread out a blanket and read all day," Kate says. I smile at her. That sounds lovely. I can see her relaxing on a blanket, hair braided, shoes off, her mind off in a different world. Kate is the kind of woman who needs a break.

"And you probably only get those days once in a great while, huh?" I ask.

She nods. "I just stay busy with school."

"Do you have a job, too?" Hunter asks.

"I work part-time at the public library and during the summers I intern at the university. The Meteorology Department has me working with airlines and sometimes I work with the military. Both jobs give me enough money to pay the bills," Kate says. Hunter gives Kate a low whistle.

"Nice. Working with the military is a hard job to land even after you get your degree," Hunter says. She's clearly impressed. "You never sleep, do you?" Kate laughs. I can't help but smile. She has a great laugh and a beautiful mouth.

"It's grueling, but I don't mind the hard work," she says. "It keeps me busy and my mind off other things."

"So this is like elementary school. Being out on the road with us. Hunter, we're going to have to impress Kate. Maybe step up our game a little."

"Oh, no, no, no. This has been incredible. Being out in it is so much better and more exciting than anything I can study in a classroom or see on video. I've been in so many different weather conditions with you two in just the four days we've spent together. A tornado, hail storms, serious flash flooding. It's been a dream of mine. I would never find the courage to do this on my own." The expression on her face is genuine and I'm trying not to feel as giddy as she looks.

"So what got you into meteorology? What do you like about it?" Hunter asks. I nod at Kate because I want to know, too. "Tristan grew up around here and her family was always into storms and her dad used to chase them back before everybody was out on the road doing this. I grew up in Arizona where there isn't much except flash floods so weather has always been fascinating." Hunter pauses, allowing Kate to form her thoughts and answer her question.

"When I was a little girl, I was always scared of storms and the thunder. My dad always told us to face our fears. He would sit with me and we would watch storms approach. We would count the seconds between lightning and thunder to see how close they were. I learned that storms were good even though they could be destructive. When you are little, you don't really pay attention to tornadoes or other weather events around the world like hurricanes and tsunamis. It wasn't until I was in high school that I really started paying attention." Kate really starts to open up when she's talking about weather. Maybe that should have been my approach all along.

"Hopefully, we can squeeze in at least one more tornado before you head back to Gage. Have you heard from him?" I ask.

"Just a few short texts. Nothing informative," she says. "I can't believe that happened to Angie. Can you imagine somebody you love getting severely hurt and it's completely out of your hands?"

"Yeah, it's awful. My boyfriend got into a wreck last year and busted his leg," Hunter says. "He was all bandaged and strung up in the hospital. It was hard to see. I couldn't help him at all."

I remember she was completely distraught. There wasn't anything anybody could do for her either. She's going to be a complete wreck when they start having kids.

"I lost my mom when I was eleven. She was in a car wreck, too. I wish I could remember her better," Kate says. Hunter and I are completely still. What do you say to that? My mom and I are very close. I don't want to think about my life without her. Growing up without a mother had to be horrible for her and the rest of her family.

"I'm sorry, Kate." I don't know what else to say. She waves her hand at me indicating it's not a big deal, but I can't imagine it not being one. "So your dad raised all of you by himself?"

"Yes. He never remarried so we all kind of took care of each other," she says.

Something big must have happened for her to be estranged from them. Even my pain in the ass brother calls me at least once a week to check in and tell me how life's going. He teases me mercilessly, but that's his way of showing love. I couldn't imagine my life without him either. This conversation really went downhill fast. I decide we need a new topic. Before I have a chance to think of something, my phone rings. It's Dr. Williams from the university. I jump up and move for privacy.

"Dr. Williams, hi. What's going on?" I ask. I feel guilty for being on a playground instead of in the SUV.

"Hi, Tristan. How's it going?" he asks. I know he's not calling to chit chat so I keep it short and sweet.

"Not bad. We have a lot of video and data already," I say. I'm quiet long enough to give him a chance to talk.

"Well, I'm afraid I don't have good news," he says. My heart sinks. I already know what he's going to say. "We didn't get the government grant this time. They aren't saying who got it yet, but the information will be released publicly in a few weeks."

"I'm so sorry, Dr. Williams. I should've tried harder or followed up with them more." I'm struggling for ground. I made the number one mistake. I assumed we had it in the bag after receiving it the last three seasons.

"It's not your fault. I should've pushed for it harder, too," he says. The blood drains from my face. My mind races, trying to figure out what to do next.

"What do we do now? Is there anything else out there for us?" I ask.

"It's late already so I'm not sure. I'll do some digging around."

"I will, too, tonight when we get to the hotel," I say. We hang up each with a plan in mind. I turn to Hunter and she knows immediately. I walk over to her.

"We didn't get it."

"I kind of figured," she says. "Who got it?"

"What's going on?" Kate asks. She looks back and forth between us.

"We lost the government grant. The grant that lets Hunter and I and the other teams go out every season and chase. Somebody else got it," I say.

Hunter falls back onto the grass. "Well, this sucks. Suddenly this perfect day isn't so perfect." I couldn't agree more.

"So what happens now?" Kate asks us.

I shrug my shoulders because I simply don't know. "I'll start looking around tonight and every night until I find something. I have a few contacts I can reach out to and see if they can help somehow." It's my responsibility to procure funds every season and I completely dropped the ball. I feel horrible for Hunter and the other teams who won't be able to head out unless we dig up some money from somewhere.

"I can't work for a television station, Tris," Hunter says. She's dead serious. She would rather bartend than work with a news crew.

"I know that. I'll figure out something." I mean it. This can't be happening again.

"I can't believe this is happening again," Hunter says. I sigh. It's on her mind, too. "You need to find out if Julie had anything to do with this."

Four years ago, I trusted a woman I was dating to keep my research of available funds and grants private, but she ended up swooping in and cashing in on all of my hard work. Since then, I've hidden anything work related from dates, girlfriends, even some colleagues.

"So what if she did? I can't do anything about it. She has access to the same grants and funding options that we do. And this grant didn't even exist four years ago so it doesn't really matter."

"Who's Julie?" Kate asks. Hunter grumbles.

"She's an ex who basically stole the funding right out from underneath me. I spent a year looking at available funds, private and public, did all the research, contacted the right people, and she went behind my back and took it all. It was hard to prove, but Hunter and I know what happened." At least I know that's not what happened this time. Hunter's the only person I trust and this hurts her even more than it hurts me. "She acted innocent and sat in front of me and everybody who questioned her and just lied."

"At least Dr. Williams believed you," Hunter says to me. "And we learned a lot about how competitive funding is."

"Yeah, we ended up scraping by the next season, using a lot of our own money, but I made it my mission to apply for every grant out there. I stay in contact with all of our financial supporters throughout the year and give them reports and updates. I'm sorry I'm whining, but our funding is a sore subject with us."

Kate nods in understanding. "I'm sorry you didn't get your grant. I'm learning just how competitive it is out in the field. You think your university is going to give you money to do what you want, but then you find out you have to go out there and get it yourself."

"Well, that just means I'll have to start from scratch and try to hit some of my old contacts," I say. I notice Hunter's shoulders slump. This is bad. I can't let her or the university down. My reputation is on the line.

Chapter Eight

Hunter put us in the best possible spot for this storm. A rural country road tucked between rows of corn and dilapidated sheds. A few cows dot the fields off in the distance. We could have been transported back one hundred years. There isn't a trace of modern life except for the telephone lines that flank the two lane highway. We pull over on the shoulder and set up video cameras. Hunter is in and out of the SUV constantly checking the pressures, wind speed, and Doppler. I can feel the energy surround us. The tiny hairs on the back of my neck are standing straight up. This is it. Kate crawls out of the back seat with her camera in hand, ready for action. I grin and point to where the clouds are beginning to swirl up above. It is very still. Too quiet. Birds aren't singing, the wind isn't blowing yet. It's the perfect recipe for a tornado. I hold my breath and wait. I'm afraid that if I say anything, it will all disappear. I've been disappointed too many times. Tornadoes don't always drop out of the wall clouds when you want them to. Today feels different. I think Mother Nature is going to deliver me one hell of a birthday gift. Of course, Hunter gets a ton of credit for getting us here, too.

"Isn't this exciting?" I turn to find Kate standing beside me. She mirrors my grin and we wait. "I've been with you for a week and I have a feeling I'm going to see another tornado on this trip."

We stand silently next to each other. I can see the goose bumps on her arm as she rubs her hand up and down for warmth. The sudden wind has dropped the temperature and the sun has disappeared behind the fast moving clouds. I reach out and rub her arm, too, and she smiles at me.

"This is why I come out here every season," I say, smiling back at her. I don't move my hand and she doesn't step away from my touch.

"Something is happening," Hunter says. Sure enough, the winds pick up, the cloud starts spinning, and the vortex dips down. I start taking photos. We see dust kicking up from the middle of the budding cornfield and Hunter and I start whooping. In a matter of seconds a thin, rope like tornado fills in the gap between heaven and earth. Kate moves closer, her finger a steady pressure on the shutter button of her fancy digital camera. We watch in awe as it thickens with dirt and debris. My ears pop and the familiar whooshing sound of a loud engine fills the air. Hunters calls it in. We watch the tornado grow. Even though it is headed away from us, we know better than to assume we are safe from it.

"Let's go!" Hunter calls.

Kate and I run back to the SUV. Even Maddox is shaking with excitement. Or fear. We drive beside it, watching it zigzag through the corn. It's a lazy tornado and doesn't seem to be going anywhere fast. We see a puff of debris. It's hit a shed or small barn.

"I hope nobody was in it," Kate says. Hunter and I mumble in agreement. Hunter stops the car ahead of the tornado so that we actually get it headed toward us instead of beside us. This is risky so I warn Kate to stay close in case it decides to chase us instead. Hunter continues to video while I snap stills. Right now, I'm so in love with Mother Nature. There is absolutely, and thankfully, nobody around us so the photos aren't cluttered with vehicles or other storm chasers. We're able to get a ton more photos and just as suddenly as it appeared, it lifts and disappears. That's the best kind. Photogenic with minimal damage. I'm so excited I feel like dancing. And the best part is that it's not raining yet. I check Doppler on the laptop just in case there are any surprises.

"That was incredible," Kate says. It looks like she is feeling the euphoric high of seeing a tornado. It never gets old and every single one is different.

"Let's go back and follow the path," Hunter says.

"Why?" Kate asks.

"If possible, we record the approximate point of contact and measure the length and width of its path if we can. Then we process the information and compare it to other tornadoes to see if there is any correlation in size, strength, and weather patterns. We don't get that opportunity often, especially since most of the time rain is close by," I say.

"But can't you figure that out based on the video?" she asks. She leans forward, her face almost directly between Hunter and me. Her eyes are wide with excitement and I notice tiny flecks of brown in them. I'm entirely too close to her. I slowly lean back and face forward in my chair again.

"It's just something we like to do. Videos are more guess work and now we have an actual touch down point to start at. The clouds are weakening and I don't think we're going to see another tornado from this system. It's nice to just verify everything," Hunter says. She's already turning the car around and we're headed back to ground zero. The rain is well off to our northeast so the soil at touchdown should still be dry. Hunter pulls the car onto the shoulder and grabs the laser measuring tool, camera, and gloves. I grab my backpack, holler for Maddox, and we climb through the barbed wire. Kate is not far behind us. Her experiences with tornadoes are minimal and this will be a valuable lesson for her. By the time she catches up to me, Hunter has already reached the initial touchdown area. "Over here, guys," she says. The budding plants have been ripped from the ground and it's not hard to follow the path. The tornado was on the ground for less than a quarter of a mile.

Maddox suddenly turns his head and perks up his ears. I know he's heard something. It's hard to hear anything over the claps of thunder off in the distance, but I know whatever he's heard, it's pretty damn important because his whole body is shaking again.

"What is it, boy?" I ask. He turns to me and barks. He runs ahead of us and turns back to us and barks again.

"Your dog is Lassie," Kate says. She's not even trying to be funny.

"Hang on, Maddox." I want him close to me because he isn't on a leash and we are on a farmstead. After experiencing a tornado, people are on edge. I can't have him be somebody's target practice. "Maddox found something," I say. Hunter looks up and nods. She knows that means I'm off and she's on her own for a bit.

"Go ahead. I've got this. Just be careful," Hunter says. Kate sticks by my side and we follow Maddox. I'm constantly calling him back to me. I can tell he's itching to let loose, but the weather is still unstable and I don't want to lose him out in a storm. He whines and I hear a soft bleating noise close by.

"Did you hear that?" I ask.

Kate turns to me, her eyes wide in alarm. "It sounds like an animal." We see a busted up pile of wood in the distance and Maddox heads toward it.

"Get back here." He obeys. I can't have him stepping on debris either. Storm chasing really isn't for dogs, but I couldn't imagine not having him by my side twenty-four seven. As we approach the heap, I see a goat on the other side of the broken structure. It's pacing back and forth and for a moment I think it's the one in distress, then I hear the bleating coming from underneath the pile. "There is something underneath that." I point and Kate and I pick up the pace. I tell Maddox to stay, my voice firm so that he knows I'm serious. We approach cautiously, the goat eyeing us warily.

"It's okay, sweetie," Kate says. "We are going to help your friend." Her voice is low and calming and for a second I stand there and just listen, the warmth of it soothing even to me. I reach into my backpack for work gloves and a flashlight. I gently lift up pieces of board and set them in a safe place. I'd throw them, but I don't want to scare the goat or whatever is underneath this pile. I see a tiny furry hoof halfway down and I pick up speed. It must be her baby. I know that I'm scaring it, but fast is the way to go now. I can't reason with it, so instead I push and slide boards away until I see more than just a hoof.

"Kate, it's her baby." She turns to me with fear in her eyes. "I need you to go into my backpack and get me the needle nose pliers. I don't think it's hurt, but it is tangled up in some wire. The boards are actually keeping it from moving around and getting cut up." Kate slowly moves away from the mama goat, still talking to it, and reaches into my bag. She hands me pliers, scissors, and a hammer. I look at her and reach for only the pliers.

"I'm sorry. I'm just nervous," she says. I wink at her.

"Don't worry. It'll be fine." I reach down and gently grab the baby goat's leg. It screams and scares the shit out of me, but I don't let go. It only takes a moment to cut the wire away from its trapped leg. I push back a few more boards and the baby goat pops out. I have about two seconds to look it over before it sees its mama and bolts. No blood. All is well.

"Oh my, God! That was incredible, Tris," Kate says. She is beaming. I'm trying to play it cool, but I really want to fist pump the sky and whoop with delight. I climb down off of the pile and watch the baby and mama goat hustle back to the farm house off in the distance. Kate reaches out and gives me a hug. I hold her for two seconds too long, but she doesn't seem to mind. "And you, too," she says, reaching down to pet Maddox on the head and scratch behind his ears. "You helped find the little guy, didn't you?"

Okay, so I'm melting right now as this beautiful woman fawns over my dog with deserved appreciation. If I can't have her attention, I'm okay with him getting it. She waves at Hunter off in the distance who is slowly making her way to us, her laser beam bouncing all over the place.

"You aren't going to believe this," Kate says, as we watch Hunter trot over to us.

"What happened?"

"Tris just saved a baby goat. Maddox heard it crying and led us over here and there was a tiny baby goat trapped under the boards and tangled up in something. Tris cut it free and now they are over there, somewhere by the farm," Kate says.

"I'm amazed the tornado didn't hit the house," Hunter says. She turns back to me and high fives me. "Congrats on the save."

I shrug and gather up the tools like something incredible didn't just happen. "Did you get what you needed?" Hunter nods.

"Do you need help?" Kate asks.

"No, thanks. I think I've got enough. Let's get off of this property before we get caught." We make a beeline for the fence, all of us excited to get back on the road.

"So what is your number one rule when chasing?" Kate asks.

I pipe up before Hunter has a chance. "Well, stay safe, make good decisions. You don't want to put yourself or others in danger for the sake of getting closer. They're so unpredictable and frightening."

"Yeah, the one I saw with Gage was intense, but I felt like he was getting entirely too close to it. I was a little scared."

"You have to be scared of it. You have to have respect for Mother Nature," I say. "She can turn in an instant. Also, the chase is over when people are in trouble. Helping them comes first."

"Do you do that a lot?" she asks.

"We are CPR certified and have helped out on occasion," Hunter says. She doesn't tell Kate how many critically injured people we've seen or helped or how we've been there for people as they wait to hear from their loved ones during storms. "There are so many more times when people have helped us out."

"What do you mean?" she asks.

"When you're out on the road and can't get out of the path of a tornado, you seek shelter. It's not a great idea to be in a car or try to outrun it. That never works out well. One time, we ran into a pizza place and all of us, the employees and diners, hid in the giant refrigerator until the storm passed," Hunter says. I smile at that recollection. The world was coming apart around us and I was thinking about the ten pound bags of mozzarella cheese within my grasp.

We reach the car and climb inside. I fire up Doppler and check things out while Hunter gets us on the road. She's right. The storm is dying out so we aren't going to see any more action from it today. There is nothing happening within driving distance either so we decide to head back to Hays, Kansas to plan our course for tomorrow. Hunter also wants to take the night off to celebrate my birthday in style. I roll my eyes. Birthdays are no longer exciting for me. Plus, the season is just getting started and we should focus more on positioning ourselves rather than celebrating. I should know better though. We do this every year.

She makes a big deal about my birthday and I pretend to hate the attention.

❖

I'm surprised to see so many people I know at the bar. I turn to Hunter and she smiles at me. Not only is she making a big deal about my birthday to our little group, but she's expanded the invitation CB style. There are about eight people at a large table already drinking beer. They toast when they see me and I wave.

"Happy Birthday, Tristan, you sexy beast," somebody says. I'm not sure who, but I feel the color rush my cheeks. I murmur a thanks and drink from the beer thrust into my hand. I see our OU partners Adam and Brian and tip my beer in their direction. Also at the table are Linda, Jo, and Chris from Texas A&M, Tammi and Anya from Oklahoma Christian University, and Bob, a lone storm chaser who is on the road simply for the thrill of seeing tornadoes. A chair is suddenly behind me and I plop down, compliments of Hunter's gentle shove.

"How old are you?" Bob asks. Tammi smacks him on the arm.

"Never ask a woman that," she says. She rolls her eyes at him and they continue their playful banter.

"I'm twenty-nine today." Adam and Brian throw a present on the table in front of me, which completely surprises me. "What's this?" I ask.

"Open it," they say in unison. I know it's a ball cap before I open it because I can feel it through the paper. The fact that they took the time to wrap it makes me smile. It's an Iowa State Cyclones cap with a red twisting bird shaped like a tornado embroidered on the bill.

"Ignore the Iowa State name," Adam says. "We picked it up last week just for you." He's proud of it and I thank them both for their generosity. Even though I don't do a lot for my birthday since I am always on the road, it's nice that others remember. Hunter doesn't disappoint. She slides a box in front of me. I don't like opening gifts in front of people, but Hunter looks like she is going to burst with excitement so I open it with vigor knowing that if I don't, she is going to lean over me and help me. It's a WindMate 300, a handheld instrument that measures everything we do, but on a much smaller and portable scale.

"This is great for when we can't get the Tahoe close enough to the tornado or when we want to confirm our readings!" She's too excited for me to remind her that my ass isn't getting that close to a tornado either.

"You're always working, aren't you, Hunter?" Kate says.

"Hey, wait a minute. Is this your girlfriend, Tris?" Bob asks. Kate smiles at him. I want to crawl under the table because I'm so embarrassed.

"I'm Kate. I'm chasing with Tris and Hunter for a few weeks." Her smile disarms the whole group. She seems very comfortable with them and I'm trying not to remember our less than fantastic meeting. Maybe it's just me. "I'm with OSU, but my chasing partner had to go home because of an emergency." She's very diplomatic. The few boos directed at OSU make her laugh. She throws a pretzel at Adam. I can't tell if she's flirting or not, but I look away. We order burgers from a passing waitress and another pitcher of beer. Everybody is talking about today's tornado and we brag a little about seeing it. Most of the teams were on the far side of the tornado and we tease them about blowing up their photos large until they see us on the nearside. We're actually having a good time and I nod my head thanking Hunter. She nods back. We aren't mushy, but there is sisterly love there. We understand each other on a completely different level. Kate tells the group the story of Maddox hearing the goat and how I saved it. Everybody applauds and I bow. It's a good night. I'm glad to have the night off with my road buddies, old and new.

"Let's dance, Tris." Brian reaches out for me and before I have a chance to protest, he pulls me up and out of my chair. Suddenly, I'm line dancing with him and about twelve other bar patrons. I don't know how to line dance. I don't even like country music, but everybody is having such a good time they're overlooking my fumbling on the dance floor. Adam wastes no time grabbing Kate. Hunter and Tammi partner up. It's a version of some electric slide dance and cowboy heel stomping. I'm so bad at it that I'm laughing and I don't even care. I'm trying to focus on keeping the fun going and less on Adam's hands all over Kate. I have no right to be jealous. "You're really bad at this," Brian says. We both laugh.

"I'm better at dancing one on one, not this line dancing and shit stomping stuff," I say. He throws his head back and laughs, drawing attention to us again. Kate and I make eye contact. It's nice to see her with a genuine smile on her face. Brian slaps his cowboy hat onto my head and we finish the awful dance. A slower song plays and we all keep our partners and start dancing the way I know dancing to be. Brian is so good sliding me around the floor that I forget I have two left feet. He twirls me away from him and then back into his arms with such ease. "I never knew you could dance," I say. Not that we would ever have the opportunity to dance at the university, but usually you learn pieces of people over time. We've been in the same department for four years and I know he's married and has a baby girl. His wife is a stay at home mom. But the dancing is new information.

"Jeannette and I don't get out much with Brianna in our lives now, but I'm going to have to make her. This is too much fun not to share," he says. I love that he loves his wife so much. The song stops and we head back to the table. I gulp down a water and nibble on some fries.

"Are you having fun?" Kate asks. She slides into the chair beside me, our legs almost touching. I can feel the heat off her and I have to stop myself from leaning into her warmth.

"Yeah, what a great night. I'm glad everybody is here and the weather cooperated," I say.

"This is a great group of friends," she says. I watch her look at them with a small smile on her face. "I thought everybody was in competition out on the road."

"That's only in the movies. To that extreme, I mean. There's competition, but we're such a small group that we're always around for each other and there isn't much room for back stabbing."

She nods in understanding. "Do you want to dance?" she asks.

I look at her in surprise. "Sure," I answer before I really think it through. She leads me out on the floor and we watch everybody to see how they're dancing before we jump in. It's a cross between another line dance and a fast waltz. Kate is very good at leading and I'm surprisingly comfortable in her arms. Granted, our bodies aren't really touching yet so it still feels fun and innocent. "How did you get to become such a good dancer?" I ask.

"I took dance classes growing up. Tap, jazz, ballroom, and some ballet."

I try not to visualize how limber she must be. "You're good at leading." Her only response is a wink. I cover my surprise with a smile.

"Hey, let me dance with the birthday girl," Adam says. He tries to whisk me away from Kate, but she holds fast to my hands. I feel her stiffen against me.

"Later, Adam. Let me finish this dance with Tristan," Kate says. He shrugs and grabs Hunter from the table instead. "He's drunk. Not quite at the obnoxious level yet, but close."

"We'll make sure he gets back to the hotel safely," I say. We're quiet for the rest of the song and, eventually, I feel Kate relax again. I don't want to ask what that was all about so instead I enjoy the last few moments of the song. Everybody claps when the music ends and immediately partner up when the first few bars of the next song plays. It's a slow song. Kate pulls me close to her and I don't question it. She always smells so good. She curls our interlocking hands between us and I almost moan when I feel the swell of her breasts against the back of my hand. Her eyes are on me the entire time and I can't look away. Her other arm is resting on my shoulder, guiding me around the dance floor. We dance back into a corner. As much as I want to joke right now to break this spell, I can't. She hasn't stopped looking at me and I haven't tried to look away.

"We should probably get back to the table," I say, noticing couples around us break apart as a new, fast song blasts through the speakers surrounding us. Kate nods and I reluctantly drop her hand. We head back to the table. Hunter looks at me and raises her eyebrow. I give her the quick I-don't-know shoulder hike hoping Kate doesn't see.

"Here's to a fantastic birthday celebration. I haven't danced or laughed this hard in a long time," Brian says. He slides into the chair between me and Kate and holds up his longneck for us to toast. "And here's to a successful and safe chase." I know he means the weather, but in my mind he means Kate.

CHAPTER NINE

The night air smells fresh and clean and I take a deep breath after stepping outside. I can only be around a group of people for so long before I need to be alone. I'm sure Maddox is going to be happy to see me. He's been cooped up in the SUV for about two hours and I'm sure he needs to expel some energy.

"How you doing, boy?" I open up the lift gate and he takes off like a bullet. I smile at his enthusiasm. I watch as he sniffs and marks his temporary territory. He trots back over to me and jumps back into the car. He stands as close to me as possible. "Too bad you can't be inside celebrating with us." I rub his nose and scratch his ears and we hug for a bit.

"How come you're out here when your party's in there?" Kate walks toward us and I can't help but admire her slender body and the slight curve of her hips. I lick my lips imagining her beneath my body, my hands touching her smooth skin, my lips tasting her. I smile because I'm sure if she knew where my mind was, she wouldn't be this sweet.

"I knew Maddox needed to run for a bit and I needed to recharge." I close the lift gate and walk around to the front to roll down the side windows for Maddox. When I close the door and turn around, Kate is very close to me. I catch my breath at her nearness. Even though it's nighttime and we're partially hidden in the shadows, I can still see her face. Her eyes are searching my face, darting back and forth between my eyes and my mouth. "What are you doing, Kate?" I ask. I don't know how I'm able to speak with her so close to me. I can feel her body heat and smell her skin and I have to stop myself from closing my eyes and getting lost in the fantasy of her nearness.

"I want to give you your present," she says.

Before I have a chance to respond, her body is flush against mine and her hands are suddenly wrapped up in my hair, her nails scraping the back of my neck. I fall back against the driver's door, the force of her body and the weakness of my knees make it too hard to hold us up. She waits only a second before her mouth captures mine. Her lips are warm and delicious and I moan when I feel her tongue touch mine. She is hesitant at first, testing my reaction. The moment she feels my hands slide down to her waist, she presses into me and boldly sucks my tongue into her mouth. Her hands leave my hair and slide down to bring my hands closer to her waist. She is aggressive, which makes my attraction to her go sky high. Usually, I'm the aggressor, but she makes me want to drop to my knees and do anything she wants.

"Kate, Kate. What are you doing?" I ask. I don't really want an answer, I just need to get ahold of this situation. I link my fingers with hers and gently push her from me. "What's going on here?"

"I'm sorry. I didn't mean to…" She tries to pull away, but I hold her fast.

"No, no. I don't want you to stop. I just want you to make sure you know what you're doing."

"You think too much, Tris. It's just a kiss." Yeah, right. I think not. That was more than just a kiss in my book. That was an 'I-need-you-now' kiss that leads to hot and heavy sex.

"If that was just a kiss, then I can't wait for more," I say. My confidence is growing and I'm starting to feel more in control. I take her hands and wrap them around my neck again. If this is my birthday present, then I sure as hell am going to enjoy it for as long as I can. I pull her back to me, sighing as her body molds against mine again. I can feel every curve and I'm surprised that I missed her warmth in the twenty seconds our bodies were apart. We kiss again, this time with more passion. Her hands trace along the waistband of my jeans and I feel her fingertips slip under my shirt to graze my bare stomach. I start quivering.

She pushes me up against the car again and this time I relent. I spread my legs so that she can get closer to me. I'm trying very hard not to reach down and pull her hard against me, wanting the hot friction of her body between my legs. I don't know if I'm going to be able to stop myself. She's a fantastic kisser and I want more. Her full mouth is soft, yet demanding and my body is burning. Just as I'm ready to reach down and slide my hand up her skirt, anxious to feel the heat of her bare skin in my hand, Maddox leans out of the window and licks the side of my face. We quickly break apart.

"Maddox! Back, now." I point to the back of the SUV and he folds his ears and slowly crawls to the other side of the seat. Kate starts shaking with laughter and I join in. "Talk about a mood killer. I'm sorry." She presses her forehead against mine.

"It's okay. I want to give you your gift before I forget," she says. I'm confused because I thought that hot make out session was my present. She opens the car door, reaches below the seat, and pulls out a brown bag. She's smiling as she hands it to me. She takes my breath away. I'm not used to seeing this carefree side of her. "I'm sorry I didn't get a chance to wrap it." I tear into the bag and she laughs at my enthusiasm. I pull out a transparent cylinder of water. She smiles at my perplexed look and takes the cylinder from me. "If you shake it, a tiny tornado forms inside.

Like this." She shakes the tube, holds it up to the moonlight and sure enough, a tornado swirls around inside for a few seconds. I smile. There is writing on the bottom of the cylinder, but it's too dark for me to make out the words. "You can read that later. I know it's kind of corny. I also want to thank you for letting me chase with you and Hunter. It's been an incredible experience."

I pull her close to me. "Thank you, Kate. It's sweet of you to think of me on my birthday."

I lean into her and kiss her softly at first, taking the time to learn her mouth, feel her lips against mine, taste her sweetness on my tongue. She presses herself into me again. I'm trying to be respectful and not strip her down in a dark, makeshift parking lot, but she's really making it difficult. I don't want to lean against the car for fear that Maddox will interrupt again so I gently push Kate back against the pickup truck parked next to us. She moans when her back hits the metal. She reaches down and rubs my upper thigh. My muscles bunch under her fingertips. She's driving me crazy.

"Kate, not here. We have to stop."

"Nobody can see us. We're completely alone," she whispers. She's staring at my lips and she's so sincere that I want to melt into her. I'm not one to fall into bed with somebody I just kissed for the first time, but her warm body pressed against me is making me rethink my morals. She's aggressive and I think we'd have more fun behind closed doors in a big bed than standing up against a rusty pickup truck in the middle of the night in Kansas. "It's okay, Tris. It's okay," she croons.

That does it for me. I move against her, devouring her mouth. She moans and I'm hoping it's because she's as turned on as I am and not because I'm too rough. At my hesitancy, she hisses a yes. I pull her skirt up until I feel the soft silk of her panties. I want to take my time, but the excitement of being out in public and the newness of her in my arms is too much and I not-so-gently tug them down. She wiggles out of them and kicks them somewhere. Her thighs are warm against my hand and I slip my fingers to her wet and swollen slit. Her arms tighten against me and she tilts her hips forward, easing my strain of trying to slip inside. I pull away to see her face as I slide one finger, then two inside of her. She bites her bottom lip and scratches my shoulder. She lifts her right leg up and puts it on the SUV behind me, giving me full access. I want to drop to my knees and bury my face into her warm pussy, but I like what we are doing too much to stop. She thrusts her hips against my hand. I pump deeper inside her.

"Oh, God, yes, Tris. Don't stop," she says.

I anchor her with my hand on her neck and shoulder, hoping I'm not marking her or holding her too tightly. She doesn't seem to mind and I stare at her in amazement as she opens herself up to me completely. Her eyes are narrow slits, but I can tell she is watching me. Her hips are moving in sync with my hand and I know she's getting close. I want to touch her everywhere and taste her, but I only have two hands and both are busy right now. Her moans are getting louder and the only way I know how to keep her quiet is kiss her.

I glide my hand under her light sweater and move my fingertips up and over her ribcage. I need to feel the sweet heaviness of her breast in my hand, feel her hard nipple between my fingertips. I peel down the lace of her bra. Even fully dressed she feels amazing. I break from kissing her and move my mouth down to her breast, biting and sucking through her sweater. Her hands grab my head and push me further into her breast. "Harder, Tris, harder," she says. She pulls her sweater up, allowing me full access. The second I suck her firm nipple into my mouth, she explodes. The sweater drops onto my face and her hands grab the back of my neck as she rocks against my mouth and my hand at the same time. It's a beautiful moment. I'm in awe of this woman.

I've had passionate interludes before, but Kate has taken me to a whole new level. I don't want to leave the sweet warmth of her body. I just got started. I know that this isn't the time or place really and what we did was in a moment of weakness. I gingerly put her bra back in place and look up at her.

She pants heavily and cups my face. "Wow."

I can't help but feel victorious. We kiss again and I gently slip out of her. My fingers are soaked with her juices. Without thinking, I bring them to my lips to taste her. I feel slightly embarrassed as she watches me. I hear her breath catch and a slight moan escape her lips and I know she's fine with it. We stand there, staring, gauging each other's reaction. I pull her into me and we hold one another for I don't know how long. I can feel the tiny shakes still rocking her body. I'm not sure what to think about what just happened. What an incredible day this has been. Saw a tornado, took great photos of it, saved a baby goat from barbed wire, and had sex against a beat up truck with a beautiful woman under a starry Kansas night.

CHAPTER TEN

You did what?" Hunter asks. We're back at the hotel, Kate in her room, and Hunter and I in ours. I sit on the end of the bed and rub my face in my hands a few times. I'm so very tired. Maddox plops down beside me, ready to go to bed.

"I went to the car to let Maddox out and she followed me. One minute she's talking about giving me my birthday present and the next we're up against a truck having hot and heavy sex." She stares at me for a full five seconds before busting out laughing.

"Casanova."

I grin and shrug my shoulders. I've never had sex when we were out chasing storms. Maybe that's it. We were coming down from the high we shared after seeing that tornado near Hays and felt the need to connect and reaffirm we survived it.

"You can't say anything." I don't know why I'm whispering or why I'm thinking we need to keep it a secret. "I mean, we didn't really talk about what happened. It might be awkward in the morning when we're all together."

"Why aren't you with her now?" she asks.

I don't know the answer. I just stare at her. I don't even know what happens now. "It's been a long day and Kate practically fell asleep at the party."

"Well, you did help her expel some serious energy."

"I don't want to go to her because I don't want her to think it's just a sex thing," I say.

"Maybe that's all she wants," Hunter says.

I don't like that. I lie on the bed and frown. I don't like that at all. Now I'm going to be awake even longer just thinking about Kate and what all of this means, if anything. Sometimes Hunter is infuriating. She's always been my voice of reason though.

"Maybe it was so good, she wants more," I say. Hunter laughs.

"Maybe so, Tris. Just don't expect anything. Keep it simple." Hunter knows I tend to dwell on things, especially when I have somebody new in my life. She's right, though. I just need to chill and wait. I roll over and close my eyes. It really has been quite the day.

❖

We aren't in any hurry to get up this morning. Yesterday was exhausting enough. Even Maddox just looks at me when I try to take him out. I slept on and off for about seven hours and I'm still tired.

"What's on the horizon?" I ask.

Hunter's hunched over her laptop. She shrugs her shoulders. "After yesterday, most of the activity is either way north or way south. There might be something happening in Oklahoma. We will just have to keep watching this system." She points to an area where two fronts, a warm one from Mexico and a cold one from the Rockies, are destined to meet. Right now, there's nothing forecast for that region, but we know how fast storms pop up. When we see a tornado, we forget about the six hundred mile days of riding in a car. We forget about greasy fast food and unsanitary bathroom breaks in the middle of nowhere. We even overlook uncomfortable catnaps in the car. Seeing a twisting rope of fury and energy from the sky erases the miserable experiences leading up to that moment.

"Let's head to Oklahoma then." I know I need to talk to Kate. I have no idea what to say though. Before I have a chance to dwell on it, we hear a knock at the door. I freeze and stare at Hunter. She lifts her eyebrow at me. I turn to the mirror and quickly primp before she opens the door.

"Good morning, Hunter," Kate says. Hunter invites her in. We make eye contact. She looks fantastic. "Good morning, Tris."

"Yes, it is, Kate," I say. We smile at each other and I swell with instant energy, the adrenaline rush of yesterday courses through my veins again. Not the tornado, but the frenzied coupling against the truck. Hunter clears her throat and I snap out of my trance. I could get lost in Kate's deep blue eyes for days. "I just need to grab some stuff out of the bathroom, then we can go."

"I'm going to let Maddox out for a bit before we hit the road. Tris, fill Kate in on what the plan is for the day," Hunter says. She grins, winks at me exaggeratedly, and gives me two thumbs up behind Kate's back. I bite the inside of my cheek trying not to laugh. Kate shuts the door and I close the distance between us.

"How did you sleep?" I ask. I don't know what else to say. I have a hundred different questions I want answers to, but this one is safe and will let me know how the rest of the conversation will go. She slides her hands up my arms and rests them gently on the back of my neck.

"I slept so well. I'm sorry I wasn't better company when we got back here," she says. She's actually apologizing to me. She gently rubs her thumb over my bottom lip then leans forward and gently kisses me. Her soft, warm mouth tastes delicious and for a split second, I want to walk her backward until we fall on the bed.

Our kiss is delicate at first, but turns passionate within moments. She moans as I slide my hands to the small of her back and pull her closer to me. I want to go lower, but we really don't have the time and reluctantly I end the kiss. I stare at her for a few moments, then brush a stray hair away from her cheek.

"Don't worry. I was pretty tired, too," I say. I didn't fall right to sleep because I kept worrying about what Hunter said. It's too soon to question Kate, so I just enjoy the feel of her body next to mine and her warm breath against my mouth. She is soft and tender against me. Her body is perfect, every curve fitting against mine. I wish it was July and we're back home where time isn't an issue and we don't have this job to do. I kiss her again because I know our private time is limited on the road.

"I enjoyed last night," she says. I'm trying not to smile arrogantly because that's not who I am. I wine and dine, I don't paw and maul and have smoking hot sex against a car.

"That's not how I usually do things," I say. She smiles against my neck. Her mouth leaves a tiny wet mark on my skin and I try not to shiver.

"It was fine, Tris. I promise." She slides her hand down the center of my chest, her fingers lightly grazing my breasts until she reaches the low waist of my jeans. I can't help but moan. "It's too bad we don't have more alone time." I wonder if it's too late to put the proverbial sock on the door. It is as I hear Hunter making a big production of coming back into the room. We break apart, but I'm still kind of holding her and she isn't pulling away. I guess we're going to be out in the open.

"You girls ready?" Hunter asks. Kudos to her for not making a big deal out of this. She grabs my bag and we follow her out to the SUV.

CHAPTER ELEVEN

We have to stop. Oh, my God," Kate says. Hunter's already trying to find a safe place for us to park. It's hard when the streets are blocked with debris. She puts on the hazard lights and we all start moving. I grab my backpack, thrust a flashlight in Kate's hand, and we head out. I'm always completely amazed at the destruction left by a tornado. There's so much going on around us that it's overwhelming and we don't know where to start. It looks like a war zone. We hear people calling so we cross the street. There's somebody trapped in a mobile home that has been tossed about thirty feet from where it was before the storm hit.

"We think Gloria is still inside." An older man is pointing to the trailer now on its side, personal items torn to bits litter the surrounding area.

"Take care of him, Kate. Hunter and I will see to Gloria." I reach into my bag and give her the first aid kit.

"Be careful," Kate says. She stares at me, her eyes wide with fear and uncertainty. I give her a weak smile and squeeze her forearm.

"I...we will." I don't want to leave her because she looks so crushed. A part of me wishes we never saw the tornado, protecting all of us from what is to become a harrowing day.

"Just call out if you need us." I turn around to find Hunter ready to start digging. She throws me a pair of leather work gloves and I slip into them, flexing them to fit me. We work quickly, moving boards and smashed personal items. I don't want to be disrespectful to Gloria, but if she's in here, finding her alive is far more important than if I crush house plants or coffee mugs. I can't feel much under my steel toe boots, but I can hear things crack as I walk around.

"Gloria!" I yell. I shine my flashlight down into crevices of lumber and insulation stacked like pick-up sticks. "Can you hear me? Are you in here?" I repeat my questions every few seconds, hoping to hear a response.

"Here! Tris, over here." Hunter waves me over, her head low to the ground. I jump down and race over to her. "I hear a knocking down here." She points to an area that looks like it used to be the kitchen. We start frantically throwing debris behind us, digging deep until we hear moaning. Eventually, we see Gloria's arm. I follow it down until I can grab hold of her hand.

"We're here, Gloria. We're going to get you out," I say. I feel a faint squeeze on my fingers and I'm reluctant to let go, but I have to if I'm going to help Hunter free this woman. "Hunter, we have to move half of this wall just to get down to her. We're going to need more help. Kate! Kate! Come here if you can," I call.

"What do you need? How can I help?" she asks. She looks pale, but determined.

"Can you see if anybody can help us? We need to move this wall to help her," I say.

"Is she okay?" she asks.

"She squeezed my hand so I know she's at least coherent, but I don't know anything else. The sooner we get her out, the better she will be."

"Okay, I'll get some help," she says. She runs off, and as much as I want to enjoy the view of Kate's backside, I have to stay focused. I turn back and continue helping Hunter, telling her Kate is going to round up some more people. Within about five minutes, Kate comes back with three young men, college age, who look as frazzled as I feel.

"There's a lady trapped down here. We need to move this wall before we can dig her out," I say. The boys nod and quickly head to the other side. They work efficiently and within about ten minutes, we're able to see more of Gloria. She is an elderly woman, and even though she is awake, I wish she wasn't. Her leg is definitely broken, judging by the unnatural angle and the metal rod sticking through her calf. I have to swallow the bile that is threatening to bubble up. Even the guys helping stop and look. I have to figure out what to do now.

"Somebody go find an ambulance or EMT. Go," I say. One of the boys jumps down and runs off. "Let's clear out as much as we can so that when he comes back with help, they'll be able to get her out immediately." I get closer to Gloria. She smiles weakly at me. I grab her hand and smile back at her. "We're going to get help. Somebody should be here very soon." I know she is in shock so I take the sweatshirt I have tied at my waist and cover her the best I can. She's mumbling something that I can't understand. I pat her hand and tell her it's okay and to relax until help comes. I can't do anything to her leg. I don't want to move it because of the break. Thankfully, her leg isn't bleeding much so I forgo the tourniquet. I don't want to do more damage than good. Hurry, hurry, hurry I chant. Within a few minutes, we hear the glorious wail of a fire truck. They can't get through because there is too much clutter, but several firemen jog over to us, carrying a stretcher. "These men are going to help you now. You can trust them." I nod to her and she nods back. I get out of the way for them to take over. My body starts to shake as my adrenaline begins to crash. Hunter stands next to me and puts her arm on my shoulder.

"Come on. Let's see if Kate needs help," she says. I know she's trying to keep my mind occupied because we both know I'm one step away from crying. I nod and we make our way over to Kate who is still comforting the old man, even though one of the firemen is attending to him.

"Hey! They need help two trailers down." One of the kids who helped us dig Gloria out is pointing to another trailer on its side. I'm completely exhausted, but I don't hesitate. Hunter jogs away and I grab Kate.

"If you want to go back to the SUV, go ahead. This is a lot to take in." I can tell she's never witnessed destruction like this before. Her body is shaking and her eyes are wide with fear.

"No, I want to help." She grabs my hand and we head to where Hunter and the boys are working. Hunter turns when she hears us.

"There's a woman with a small boy and a baby in here. She's probably in the bathroom, but we don't know for sure. We can't get the door open so we're going to climb in through the skylight," Hunter says. I can only nod. Hunter turns to Kate and holds her forearms. "Kate, we can hear crying. That's a good sign." Kate starts crying, but nods to let Hunter know that she understands. "I'm going to climb up and see if I can help from up there. Why don't you two try to find dry blankets or towels, okay?" I love that Hunter is a leader. I hand Kate the car keys.

"We have a few extra stadium blankets in the back next to Maddox's toys. Can you run and get them?" She nods and runs toward the SUV. I know she needs to get away from this, even if it's just for a minute or two to regain composure. I can see Hunter and a college boy working on the skylight. I take the two other boys and we walk around the trailer trying to find another way in. We have to walk around broken tree limbs and debris. Our only option is to break a window if Hunter is unsuccessful.

"Up here. We're in," she yells to me. I give her a thumbs up. We wait as she slips inside. I can hear her calling out and see the whip of the flashlight beam bounce from one side of the trailer to the other. What feels like hours is only a few minutes. I feel completely helpless standing around so I climb up and peek inside, shining my flashlight right into Hunter's eyes.

"I can hear a woman and a baby. They're trapped inside the bathroom and can't get the door open. I have to move a table and the stove from the door," she says. She's getting drenched with water spewing from where a sink used to be.

"You need help?" She nods and heads over to me. I slip down and she grabs my hips. I land not so gently on dishes and piles of stuff.

"Careful, Tris. I can't have you hurt, too." She steadies me and turns her attention back to the bathroom. The two of us are able to move the stove out of the way and get the bathroom door open. I'm afraid of what we're going to find. There's a woman sitting on the floor, her head and shoulders protecting a baby nestled on her lap. She blinks at the flashlight and I quickly shine it elsewhere. The woman has a cut on her arm and forehead, but she seems to be in good shape otherwise. The baby, thankfully, is completely unharmed. Mad as hell, but healthy.

"Where's Robert?" she asks. Hunter looks at me. I back out of the bathroom and start looking for Robert, who I assume is the young boy the neighbor told us about. I shine the flashlight all over, but I can't find him. He's not answering me either, but I'm sure he is too frightened to speak or come out of hiding.

"I can't find Robert, ma'am. Was he with you in the bathroom?" I ask. She starts crying. Hunter does her best to calm her down.

"We'll find him. He's probably a smart little boy and is still hiding," Hunter says. "In the meantime, we need to get you and the baby out of here and get you help." She looks at the front door, but it's completely warped and won't budge. "Is there a back door or another way out of here?"

"There's a trap door. It goes under the trailer. We can try that," the woman says.

So everything that was in front of the bathroom door that we tossed aside, now has to be moved again. It takes us a few minutes, but we're able to clear the area off of the door in the floor. Hunter opens the door and gasps.

"Are you Robert?" she asks. Under the trap door is a little boy, about seven-years-old. He is dirty and bruised, but seemingly okay. He doesn't start crying until he sees his mother. That gets the baby crying, too. "Okay, listen. We're all going to have to crawl out of here, but we need to be careful. The trailer has moved so the blocks aren't as sturdy. This is the quickest way out. The sooner we get out, the sooner Robert can tell us about his adventure." Hunter turns to Robert. "Can you show us the way out?" At his enthusiastic nod, she takes off her headlamp and puts it on his head. He smiles and scurries out like it's a game. It's going to be tricky with a baby.

"I can hold the baby and slide out on my back," I say. I know the mom must be exhausted and this seems like the safest way to get everyone out.

"Be careful with her," the mom says.

"I promise." I put on Hunter's jacket for protection and carefully crawl down into the space. Hunter hands me the baby. She's whining, but not crying now. I clutch her to me and scoot out as quickly as possible. The boys are waiting for us and scoop us up. Within a few minutes, the family is together again. Hunter and I carefully check them for injuries. The mom received the brunt of the injuries with a three inch gash on her arm and a cut on her forehead. Robert has scrapes and bruises, but nothing that requires any medical attention. The baby is surprisingly quiet and we wrap her up in a blanket that Kate hands the mom. She thanks us over and over again. By now, the area has grown with volunteers and firefighters, so we know it's okay to leave it in their capable hands.

"I sure hope everybody is going to be okay," Kate says as we make our way back to the SUV. I let Maddox out and make sure he stays close to me. He's aware things are bad and is quick to do his business. We all climb into the car and Hunter carefully maneuvers us around fallen trees. I'm glad it's dark because if I see the destruction right now, I will break down. Kate's already in the back seat crying and I don't know how to comfort her. Maddox is trying, but it's not working.

"Those poor people," she says. "What happens now? What are they going to do?" The first time you see the devastation left by a tornado firsthand, it changes you. After six seasons of doing this, it doesn't get any better, but it's less shocking. Hunter and I are silent. We don't have the answers.

After about twenty minutes of driving, we find a motel and drag ourselves into the room. We take turns in the bathroom cleaning up. Within half an hour, we're ready for bed.

"I don't want to sleep alone," Kate says. Hunter and I are in one bed and I don't even hesitate. I crawl into the other bed and Kate snuggles into me. I hold her close, the warmth of her body comforting. I can feel her body shaking and I know she's crying again. After a few minutes, she relaxes. We fall asleep entwined and I'm grateful for such a tender end to a horrible day.

CHAPTER TWELVE

G age said Angie is doing better. She's going home so he should be back in action Thursday." Kate puts her phone back in her pocket. We're all still dazed from Sunday's tornado so good news is welcome. "That gives me a few more days of chasing with you ladies." I smile at her. I've really enjoyed having her with us. Not just because we had sex, but because it's nice to have a professional connection and be with somebody who is just as excited as I am about weather.

"Then we should plan accordingly," Hunter says. "Let's have girls' night out tomorrow and play like we're back in civilization. Eat a nice, expensive dinner, maybe go shopping first. Oh, or go see a movie." We all smile. "How long has it been since we let loose?"

"I don't even know," I say. Kate smiles at me. Okay, so maybe a few days ago. I smile sheepishly back at her and run my hands through my hair. I'm self-conscious again. "Let's do it." I'm actually excited. It will be nice to get dolled up and go out for a night. "I think we all could use a break." My wardrobe is lacking, but I'm sure I can find something decent. If not, I can buy something when we go shopping.

We're chasing near Lawrence, Kansas and we decide to just stay in the quaint college town. We don't know much about the movies that are out, so we plan on a concert instead. Dar Williams is playing at Liberty Hall and there is an excellent restaurant just a few blocks up from the venue. I'm considering this a date even though Hunter will be with us. I'm itching to get my hands on Kate, away from our job and Hunter, and just have hours of me and her without interruption. Plus, she's leaving us and I can't let her go without touching her at least one last time.

I'm taking Hunter's advice and just going with the flow. Whatever happens, happens. Kate is four years younger than I am and when you're in your twenties, the difference in age is vast. She's probably fresh out of her sorority and I've been a cynic since birth. I have a need to show her that I can clean up and function like a perfect lady. She's used to stubby ponytails and jeans that I wear for days without washing. She doesn't know that the other nine months out of the year I wear skirts and makeup and file my nails instead of biting them. I have this incredible urge to please her.

"I told Gage that I'll let him know where we'll be and he'll come up and get me," Kate says.

"It's been nice having you around. I know Maddox likes having a backseat buddy," Hunter says. I have a thousand things I'd like to say to her, but everything sounds stupid. We have so many things to talk about.

"I might have to dognap him when nobody's looking," Kate says. She reaches over and scratches his chest and he leans against her. Hey, I thought only I got his hugs.

"He has a lot of baggage, you know," I say.

"Yeah, an overprotective mother," Hunter says.

"And an overprotective aunt," I say. We smile at one another. Both of us would do anything for Maddox. During off season, I swear Hunter only comes by to visit Maddox.

"Why does he have these scars?" Kate asks. I watch as her fingertips trace the patterns of slightly puckered and white skin.

I tell her, but I try to keep it as tactful as I can. We've already been through a lot this week and I don't need her to be sad for Maddox, too. He is the best thing that has happened to me and I want her to be happy for him as well. "Well, he's beautiful and I'm sure he doesn't even remember what happened that long ago." She kisses the side of his head and he falls down in her lap. He's so obvious and I'm so jealous. I might have to steal his signature move.

❖

I'm not one to brag, but I look hot tonight. In all fairness, I did spend a great deal of time primping. Even Hunter whistles when I walk out of the bathroom. I'm wearing a cute little black dress I picked up at a vintage clothing store up the street from our hotel. My hair is wavy and I'm accentuating my bedroom eyes with just enough eyeliner and mascara. To top things off, I'm even wearing heels.

"You're dressed to get laid tonight," Hunter says. Am I that obvious? Good.

"I don't look whorish, do I?" I'm suddenly nervous. Hunter walks over and puts her hands on my shoulders.

"You look fantastic. I mean gorgeous, actually. If she doesn't take advantage of you, I just might." She winks at me and does a little twirl herself for attention. She looks great as well. She is wearing new jeans, a button-down oxford, and badass Doc Martens.

"You look very dapper tonight."

Hunter likes dressing preppy. I refrain from calling her handsome because she doesn't like that, but if she crossed over to my side, she would be so very popular with the ladies. She bows and reaches out to me. I slide up to her and she holds me like we're dancing. We waltz until Maddox decides he wants to be part of the action and jumps up on us. We laugh and break apart.

"Let's go find Kate and have a fantastic time," Hunter says. We say good-bye to Maddox and go to meet Kate in the lobby. Her room is upstairs, but our room is ground level and tucked in the back like always. I'd leave Maddox in the car if I thought he would be safe, but since we are in town, I don't want people to mess with him. The room will be quiet and comfortable enough.

I try not to look at Kate as we walk down the hall toward her. I can't help it though. She looks incredible. She, too, is wearing a dress. It's longer than mine, but a lot tighter. She has an amazing body. I know this already, but tonight there isn't much to imagine or remember. I just need to look.

"Wow, look at you ladies," Kate says. She looks us up and down and motions for us to twirl. "No Neanderthals here."

"I told you I clean up," I say. I'm trying not to be smug, but it's hard when she's looking at me appreciatively. I refrain from reaching out for her and saying 'yummy' because that would definitely make me a caveman. No, tonight I shall behave like a lady. At least until it's time to say good night.

"The weather is perfect. No rain and nice warm temperatures," Kate says. Since everything is so close, we decide to walk to the restaurant and the concert. I sort of regret that decision because these heels are killing me. Oh, the pain and suffering to please a girl. The restaurant is an old converted bank building. We start off with a bottle of wine and toast Kate, wishing her well on her return back to OSU and Gage's tutelage in the field. She seems a little sad, but she toasts with us. "Thank you, ladies, for taking me in and showing me the good and the bad of storm chasing. It has been an honor." She sips her wine, her eyes never leaving mine. A little shiver works its way through my body and I smile at her with anticipation. I so can't wait until we get back to the hotel.

We eat our meals and recap our short time together. Kate tells us what she originally thought of us and how she feels about us now. "I was actually kind of afraid of Hunter," she says. We laugh. It's not the first time we've heard this.

The venue is fantastic even though our seats are on the second level. Hunter's on my left and Kate's on my right. Kate slides her hand into mine the minute we sit down. I'm so happy it's hard to stay still. I turn and give her a smile. Hunter nudges me and I look at her. She raises her eyebrow and I lift my shoulder slightly. I don't know what's going on, but I'm just going to go with it. Kate's fingers are warm curled around mine. I almost bring her hand up to my lips, but stop myself in time. We aren't there yet. When our hands break apart to clap after each song, she finds my hand again when the applause ends. It's very sweet.

We stay the entire concert. Afterward, Hunter tells us she's going to hang back and get Dar's signature. She tells us to go on without her.

"Are you sure?" I ask.

Hunter leans close to me and whispers, "I'll take care of Maddox. Go have a good time." She squeezes my waist and I smile at her.

I walk over to Kate. "We've got the rest of the night to ourselves. Hunter is going to take care of Maddox then hit the hay."

"We could grab a drink somewhere. There's a bar on every corner."

We decide on a little tavern just a few doors down. We can hear jazz playing and the music entices us to enter. Surprisingly, there aren't too many patrons. We grab a quiet booth near the side of the stage that is partially hidden in the shadows of the upper level. Perfect for a respectable amount of privacy.

"So when do you stop chasing?" Kate asks.

"When the weather stabilizes. Usually near the end of June. Aren't you going to be with Gage that long, too?" I ask.

She shakes her head no. "I'm only on the road for one more week, then another meteorology student gets to ride with him. I'm still in school. As much as I would like to finish out the storm chasing season, I have to get back to my other classes."

"They let you miss classes for this long?" I ask. Most universities don't allow that unless the student is exceptional and has presented them with a killer idea or educational plan.

"I used my charms," she says. She doesn't want me to know the real reason, so I let it go. Instead I smile at her. Nothing is going to ruin this night.

"Good for you. That alone is a big accomplishment."

We order drinks and listen to the band play. Kate slides closer to me so that our legs are touching. She leans her head on my shoulder. I'm afraid to move, even breathe, in case she moves away. She runs her fingertips down my arm and gives me chills instantly.

"Are you cold?" she asks.

"I'm just enjoying your touch." Might as well be honest.

"Well, in that case…" Her voice trails off and I'm intrigued. Her fingertips trace my arm again, but this time they continue down until I feel their warmth on my leg. I look at her and she smiles at me. She twirls her fingers lightly on my leg, drawing little designs. My breath catches when her fingers find their way under my dress near the knee. "You are so soft, Tris." Her voice is low, almost raspy and my passion for her instantly flares.

Her fingertips tease me, moving higher, running along the line where my left leg is crossed over my right. I uncross my legs. I have no shame. We're secluded and nobody can see what she is doing to me under the table. She moves her fingertips to the inside of my thighs and I catch my breath. My lips part and I try to control my breathing. She's teasing me and I'm thoroughly enjoying it. I move my arm and place it across her shoulders. It seems like a sweet gesture, but I'm only doing it so that she'll move closer to me. She takes the hint and presses up right next to me. She sits up straighter, moving her hand away from my legs. I frown. She leans over and kisses the corner of my mouth. She crosses her right leg over her left and tilts her body closer to mine. "I'm just getting closer to you." She slides her hand back to where it was, only this time she pulls my legs apart further than they already are. I can feel my nipples harden at her aggressiveness. She rests her chin on my shoulder and watches me while her fingers continue their torturous seduction. She moves higher and higher until she lightly grazes the lace of my panties. I almost jump at the contact. "I think you like this, Tris," she says. I can't look at her because she is so close so I nod instead.

"Very much," I say. I can feel her smile against me. I gasp when she runs her fingers up and down, applying pressure in all the right places.

"Shhhh. People are going to know what we're doing," she says. "You have to be quiet." Easy for her to say. Giving up control is so hard, but the reward is so good. I want to touch her, too, but I can't move. I'll just have to wait until we're alone. When she tries to slip her fingers inside of my panties, I throw in the towel.

"Let's go," I say. I push myself away from her and stand, straightening my dress. Every part of my body is on fire and we only have a few hours left before Kate's gone. I throw a twenty on the table and reach for her hand. She smiles almost smugly at me and slips her hand into mine. I don't even care that my heels are pinching again. I want to get back to the hotel room. I want my time alone with Kate. We walk to the hotel in silence, our fingers still entwined. The hotel is only a block away. We're so close and I wonder if we're even going to make it. Kate is walking just as fast as I am so I know she wants this, too. No regrets, I tell myself. Just enjoy the moment.

I hold the door open for her and head for the elevators. Unfortunately, another couple decides to ride the elevator up with us so our contact remains PG. Kate digs around for her key card as we walk to her room. When the key opens the door and she pushes down on the handle, I push against her to get into the room faster. I grab her and kiss her until her back is up against the closet door. She reaches to pull up my dress, but I stop her and snake her arms up over her head. I break the kiss and stare at her. I look at her face, her swollen lips, her nipples straining against the already tight dress. I remember what it was like to taste her skin.

"Please, Tris, hurry," she says. Her voice is tight.

"Oh, no. Tonight, we're going to take it slow." I lean into her and capture her mouth in a searing kiss that makes us both moan. I pull her with me as I walk backward until I feel the mattress hit my legs. I turn with her in my arms and we fall onto the bed. She wraps her hands in my hair, pulling me even closer. Her dress prevents me from sinking between her legs so I roughly push it up. She lifts her hips to help me. I remind myself to slow down. We've already done this the rough way. Tonight, I want gentle. I take the time to touch her everywhere, unhurriedly. I unbutton the front of her dress and run my fingers along her collarbone, the smoothness of her skin softer than silk. I follow the same path with my mouth and almost cry with joy when I taste the sweetness of her breast, the rough texture of her nipple against my tongue. Her hands tighten in my hair and she pushes me into her. I run my fingertips over her other breast, gently squeezing her pebbled nipple. She moans again, louder, the sound sends goose bumps up and down my body. I love that she is so passionate.

"Please take off your dress, Tris," she whispers. "I need to feel you against me." I lean up and she helps me lift the dress up and over my head. I reach out for her dress and take that off, too. She isn't wearing a thing underneath. I'm so thankful I did not know that four hours ago. I never would've survived our dinner or the concert. She is slender and pale and lovely. The lights aren't on, but the drapes are open so we have plenty of light filtering into the room.

"You're beautiful, Kate." I lean forward for another kiss. She reaches around and unhooks my bra, sliding the straps down my arms. I shudder at the coolness of the room and the tenderness of her touch. Her hands slide down my stomach until they reach my panties.

"You're the beautiful one, Tristan. Your body is strong and lean and still soft in all the right places." She's being tender and I have to tell myself not to cry. The way she is touching me, as if trying to memorize me, is too much to handle. I can't think about why. I just need to be close to her. I cup her face in my hands and kiss her, moving closer until we are completely flush against one another. Her body is so warm and I can feel her surrender to me. We lie down and I move to the side so that I'm not completely on her, but our legs are entwined.

I want to touch and taste her everywhere. She faces me and we continue kissing as I trail my fingertips over her neck and shoulders. Her lip quivers when my fingertips get closer to her breasts. I break the kiss and watch her as my hand closes over her breast. Her eyelids flutter shut and her mouth opens as she gasps softly. I lean down and place tiny kisses across her body until my mouth reaches her breast. I gently flick her nipple with my tongue before I suck as much of her into my mouth as I can. Her hands rest on the back of my neck, scratching me gently, but firmly. Her hips start moving against me like she is trying to find friction. I slide my hand down until I reach the junction of her thighs. As much as I really want to go slow, I just can't wait anymore. Time is our enemy. She will be gone tomorrow. She is wet and I slip into her, easily and deeply. She arches her back and cries out with pleasure. Her mouth finds mine and she kisses me with a touch of desperation. She reaches out to me and I cover her body with mine. My hand is still between us, giving her pleasure, moving against her hips. She spreads her legs further apart, her body tensing for release. I decide I really don't want to be this quick so I slow my movements. Our whirlwind sex against the truck the other night was fantastic, but I want tonight to come more from the heart and less from my libido.

"I need to taste you," I say when she looks at me in confusion. I begin a trail of kisses from her neck, down the valley of her breasts, over her flat stomach to the soft curls on her mound. Her fingers wound in my hair, pull me gently, push me softly. I smile at her eagerness.

"Tris, you're driving me crazy," she whimpers. Not one to disappoint, I spread her apart and run my tongue up one side and down the other, careful not to touch her clit just yet. She moans again, this time her voice is deeper, thickening with passion. "Please." I slip two fingers inside of her and begin moving slowly, allowing her to stretch and adjust to me. It doesn't take long because she is so wet. Her hips start moving against my hand. She's not a talker, but her body is speaking to me. I know exactly what to do and how to do it. I find her clit with my tongue and start moving my hand. Her moans are getting louder and that only encourages me to be a bit more aggressive. I stroke her harder, speeding up only when she asks for it. She grabs her breasts and squeezes her nipples every time I lick. I decide I've taken enough time and I should give her what we both want. I build her up again, but this time I keep going and she crests beautifully. Her back arches off of the bed and I place my hand on her thighs to keep her from falling off. She shakes. A light film of sweat covers her body and I'm in awe of her again. Kate isn't afraid to embrace her orgasms. She isn't quiet or ashamed and it's so refreshing. I climb back up her body, licking her salty sweat wherever I place a kiss. She surprises me by wrapping her arms around me and holding me close while her body continues to ride the aftershocks. I sink into her, kissing her neck until she can breathe normally again.

"I was right," I whisper in her ear. She turns her head to me.

"About what?" She is still short of breath.

"You really are beautiful," I say before I kiss her. She makes some sort of negative noise so I playfully bite her bottom lip. "Trust me. I know." She growls and I release her lip, only to have it back against my mouth within a second as she leans up and kisses me again. This time, she pushes me over so that I'm flat on my back. I love this aggressiveness. She looks so delicate, but she has repeatedly surprised me with her forceful nature. I like giving up control with her. She slides over me and tilts her head so we are eye to eye. I can feel her wetness on my leg. I lick my lips wanting to taste her again. She arches her brow at me and I smile. "And you taste amazing." Her hair is curtained around us. I grab some and smell. "And smell wonderful." For a moment, she looks sad. "Hey, come here." I pull her down to me and kiss her. She doesn't waste time getting to know my body. Her hands move down my torso, stopping at my curves, feeling them over and over. I greedily spread myself for her. She settles between my legs and I cup her ass and press her into me. We both moan at the contact. I'm not a selfish lover, but it's been so long and Kate's so sexy that I know I'm not going to last. I reach down between us to ease the ache of my throbbing clit, but she stops me.

"What are you doing?" she asks. She stops my hand and brings it up above my head. "Don't move." I can't help but smile at her. This time she smiles back, the sadness gone. She moves my other hand up, too, and commands that I not move them under any circumstances. She leans down and kisses me softly, first on my lips, then my cheek, and finally my earlobe. She bites down on the soft flesh and I tense up as pleasurable spikes of pain radiate throughout me. I shiver and moan. She moves down to my neck and I lean to the side to give her more room. She starts off kissing me softly, then she starts sucking. I almost come just from that incredible feeling. I lift my hands up briefly and she stops again. "Ah, ah, ah. No, no," she says. I whisper an apology and she continues. I don't even care that she might be leaving marks. She moves further down and I whimper at the loss of her lips against my neck. She reaches my breasts and runs her mouth softly over them, her tongue flicking out to tease my nipples. I hate that I can't touch her right now. As much as I want to flip her and taste her again, curiosity wins out. I want to know what she has in mind for me. Her hair tickles me as her journey across my body continues. She rubs my stomach, feeling my abs. I silently thank Hunter for dragging me to the gym every day after work. "You're the one with the perfect body. So strong and curvy." She straddles me.

"Can I please touch you?" I ask. My hands are almost fists now. I'm desperate to hold her.

"I kind of like you like this," she says. "But it's only fair that you get to touch me, since I got to touch you." That's all she needs to say. I sit up with her on my lap, surprising her. I flip us so that I'm once again on top. "Hey," she says. I respond with a kiss. This time she is the one who snakes a hand between our bodies and starts rubbing my swollen pussy. I moan loudly against her cheek and start grinding myself against her hand, against her entire body. It doesn't take me long to come. I grit my teeth and try hard not to cry out because my mouth is right next to her ear. I can't remember the last time I had an orgasm. I feel fantastic. I don't want to crush her, so I gingerly roll to the side. She keeps her hand between my legs and watches me as her fingers continue to move inside of me. She draws out another orgasm, which catches us both by surprise. This time I'm not quiet. She moans as I come, watching me rise and fall with each wave of ecstasy. I curl up in a ball until I can relax.

She leans over me, whispering words I can't understand, but I sigh contently when she places tiny kisses on my ear. I could get used to this. I stretch back out and pull her closer to me. We don't speak. We just lie there, looking at one another. I reach out and touch her cheek and tuck her hair behind her ear. She smiles and leans down to place a kiss on the palm of my hand. It's so tender and sweet I feel a tiny tear slip out of the corner of my eye. I have to cover or else she'll see it.

"Come here. Let's snuggle," I say. She curls up with me and I hold her. I'm going to miss her. Hunter and I still have at least six more weeks on the road. Kate will be going back to school in a week and then I won't get the chance to see her for who knows how long. Plus, I don't even know what she wants so I have to play it cool like Hunter said. I pull the covers over us and nuzzle her neck. Even sweaty, she's perfect in my arms.

❖

I wake up with Kate's head on my shoulder. My phone is buzzing. I'm surprised the noise doesn't wake her. I grab the phone. It's Hunter. No way am I answering it right now. I shoot her a text instead.

Is everything okay?

She fires back a message.

Perfect. Just checking in. What time are we hitting the road?

I look at the time and am surprised that it's already eight.

Let me wake up Kate but I'm thinking ten. Give me some time.

She sends me a happy face emoticon and I chuckle. Kate stirs next to me. Apparently, we woke her anyway.

"Good morning," she says. It's more of a mumble, but I'm pretty sure that's what she says. I kiss the top of her head and she snuggles closer to me.

"Good morning."

"Is everything all right?" she asks.

"Hunter just wanted to know what time we want to leave today."

"Can she wait until it's an acceptable time?" she asks. I laugh and show her the time on my phone. She sits up immediately and turns to face me. "It's already eight? But we just fell asleep."

"About six hours ago," I say.

She looks around in disbelief. "That's so not fair." She lies back down and pulls the covers over us.

"I'm going to shower, but you stay here and get some more sleep. I'll wake you when it's the last possible second, okay?" I crawl out of bed and head for the bathroom. I'm not happy we are parting today either, but we both have responsibilities. A few minutes later, the bathroom door opens and Kate comes in.

"Is it okay if I shower, too?" she asks. A beautiful naked woman is standing on the other side of the shower curtain wanting to get close to me again. I can't get her into the shower fast enough. She giggles at my playfulness and I rotate us so that she is under the hot stream. "Mmmm. This feels heavenly." I watch as she wets her long hair. Her head is tilted back, her eyes closed and her body slick. Seeing her in the light is breathtaking. The water cascades down her body, gliding over her breasts. Her glistening nipples beckon me. I lean forward and kiss one then the other. I feel her fingers thread in my hair, guiding me closer to her body. "We're never going to get out of here on time if you keep doing this," she says.

"I can stop," I say.

"No way." She holds my face in her hands and kisses me. It's a deep, passionate kiss that leaves us both breathless and wanting more. I know we don't have time, but I also don't know when I will have Kate all to myself again in a nice hotel room. My passion wins and I push her back up against the wall, needing her against me, wanting her inside of me again. I balance my leg up against the side of the tub and watch as her hand runs the length of my thigh before she easily slips two fingers inside of me. I pull her close to me and kiss her hard, moaning against her mouth as her hand presses into me. She breaks the kiss and slides down until she is on her knees in front of me. I don't stop her. I don't break eye contact until she spreads me and I feel her wet, hot mouth on my clit. I close my eyes and allow the rush of our passion to fill me. I selfishly put my hand on the back of her head, partly to steady myself and partly to hold her in place. I come quick and hard. She stands, smiling at me until I pull her into another hot kiss. We are both still breathing heavy when we break apart.

"Hurry up with your shower," I say. I slip out before she can protest further. I dry off and wrap the towel around my body. I realize I don't have any of my clothes and I'm not about to wear the same dress from last night. I grab my phone and text Hunter.

Kate's in the shower. Can you bring me some clothes real quick?

I only have to wait ten seconds before she responds.

Look outside the door.

I open the door and see a bag of my stuff. I fucking love Hunter. She thinks of everything.

You're my favorite person in the world. See you at ten.

I hear the shower turn off and I panic for no reason. Should I stay in my towel? Do we have time for another round of sex? Is she even up for another round? Should I just get dressed? Before I even have time to answer myself, Kate opens the door and peeks out.

"Was somebody at the door?"

"Hunter dropped off a bag for me since all I have is my stuff from last night," I say.

"You aren't really going to get dressed yet, are you?" she asks.

"Well…"

"Don't move from that spot," she says. She closes the bathroom door for just a few seconds before coming out wearing a towel, too. "What time is it?"

"Eight thirty."

She walks over to me, her towel precariously close to falling down.

"That gives us at least an hour before we have to really get ready, unless you want to leave now…" Her voice trails off as she plays with the hem of my towel. I grab her towel and pull her flush up against me.

"I don't want to leave without tasting you again," I say.

She looks at my mouth and runs her thumb along my bottom lip. "You have a very nice mouth."

I lean and kiss her gently. She drops her towel and pulls mine, too, so that we are both naked. She's still wet from the shower and she shivers against me. I pull her closer and walk her over to the bed.

"Get in," I say. She crawls in and I quickly follow. I cover her with my body and she moans.

"You're so warm," she says. I'm always warm. We start kissing again. I spend the next hour memorizing her body until we're forced to leave the sanctuary of blankets and get back on the road.

❖

"Be sure to check in with us. We'll send you any photos we get of massive tornadoes," Hunter tells Kate. She gives her a quick hug and heads over to Gage, giving us a few private moments. Since Gage missed most of the allotted time with Kate, the university extended her time by a week.

"Be careful, okay? Don't let him do anything stupid," I say, pointing my thumb at Gage.

"I'll make sure he's safe," she says. She steps closer and looks around before placing a quick kiss on my already swollen lips. "Thank you for letting me ride with you both. And thank you for last night. I hope that I get to see you when you are done chasing." I can't help but grin. This is the first time she's mentioned the future.

"Definitely," I say. I twirl her hair one last time and climb into the SUV. Maddox hangs his head out of the window and Kate nuzzles him.

"I'm going to miss you, too, Maddox. Be good to mama, okay, boy?" she says. He licks her face and she laughs. Hunter climbs into the driver's seat and we wave to Kate and Gage.

"Thanks again, guys," Gage says. I was happy to find out that Angie is doing better and her mother is staying with her to help her get around while Gage returns to work. We pull out, waving to them as we pass.

Hunter reaches over and squeezes my arm. "I'm happy for you."

I smile. I'm happy for me, too. "She's really great. Smart, funny, sexy. And she wants to see me when we are done for the season."

"Why are you acting so surprised? You're great, you know," Hunter says. "I mean, she's great, too, but you deserve this." Hunter has been after me to date forever now. She's been there for me through the bad dates, the good ones, the quick break-ups and the ones that took forever to shake off.

"Well, hopefully, this one will have a good ending." I stare out of the window and think about Kate. She's everything I've ever looked for in a partner. I know she's private, but I hope that with time and support, she will open up to me and reveal why she has a heavy heart some days.

CHAPTER THIRTEEN

Funny how I'm not in the mood to chase today. The girl, yes, the weather, no. I feel like I didn't have enough time with Kate. We've been texting and sharing a few words on the CB radio, but nothing emotional. Maybe that was it. Our time together was just for fun. She is young and just getting started with her life. I feel like a whiny, clingy girlfriend right now. I sigh.

"Quit it," Hunter says. I look at her like I don't know what she's talking about, but she just gives me a look. I don't even try to hide it.

"So that was it? Just sex?" I ask her.

"What do you want? A ring already? Come on, Tris, you've got to give it some time. Maybe she's not open and doesn't want a lot of people knowing. You can respect that, right?" She makes a good point. I don't know if Kate is in the closet at work or at home so I need to settle down and quit feeling sorry for myself. "Plus, didn't she say she wanted to get together when we're done? That's only in seven or eight weeks."

"I guess I just wanted more alone time with her. You know how I get."

"Do not blow this. Just roll with it. See where her head is. She's very cool and perfect for you. Don't do anything stupid." Hunter knows I don't do casual, so this is hard for me. I just never understood casual. I get emotionally tangled up in a woman and then stifle her with my neediness. Hunter and I have talked about this and I have given her full permission to kick my ass when I start acting like a high school girl. She's about ready to.

"This is what happens when I go too long between dates." I'm groaning now. "I don't even remember the last girl I dated. When was the last time I had sex before Kate?"

"That crazy girl you met last fall at Helen's party. Wasn't her name Anna or something?" Hunter snorts remembering that whole ordeal. I chuckle with her.

"Yeah, that was kind of messed up, huh?" I say.

"Are you fucking kidding me right now?" Hunter's laughing so hard, she's pounding the steering wheel. "You practically had to gnaw off your arm to get away from her. And then when I had to pretend to be your jealous ex-girlfriend who wanted you back. You still owe me for that. I'm so happy she stopped coming around." We've all either had stalkers or been one. She was my official stalker. At first I thought it as all harmless, like puppy love, but then she started showing up at my job and I had to end it. Hard. I spent most nights at Hunter's place until she finally got the hint.

"Well, I somehow don't think Kate is like Anna," I say.

"I'm saying don't be like Anna to Kate."

Well, that's eye-opening. I nod my head and look out the window. Suddenly, it's not funny anymore. "I won't. I think I've only expressed my craziness to you," I say. Hunter nods and reaches for my ponytail stub and gives it a quick tug. I smack her hand away.

"I don't think we're going to see too much today. We've been real lucky the last few weeks so maybe our luck is running out," I say. Since Kate left four days ago, we haven't seen a single tornado. The storms have been rather weak and not holding up well.

"We've never had such a volatile start before. I mean, in one day we saw four tornadoes. That rarely happens. And two in one wall cloud. Just crazy."

"It's been great, hasn't it?"

"I can't wait until we can go back and analyze all of this data and watch the videos." This is Hunter's ideal job. I feel even worse for failing to get the grant. Shit. I need to do something.

"Look, Hunter, I'm going to try really hard to get us money. I'm sorry I dropped the ball on the grant."

"It's not your fault, Tris. It's not your decision. You did everything you were supposed to do. Somebody else just did it better." She shrugs her shoulders as if it's not a big deal, but I know it bothers her. How can it not?

"Since nothing is happening outside, I'll just fire up the laptop and start digging around. Not too many people have responded to my e-mails. Don't you have a rich uncle or something?" I ask. Hunter laughs.

"If that was the case, I'd do this on my own without OU."

"Without me?" I'm kind of surprised.

"Well, I would want you there, but you can't leave OU. Your whole life is the university." She's got a point. I even have a couch that pulls out into a bed in my office. You would think I'm finding a cure for cancer with as many hours as I spend in the lab.

"Hey, if your rich uncle wants to give me money to drive around the country chasing tornadoes, I would leave OU in a heartbeat."

"You love teaching too much. And you're good at it. You stay put," she says. "Besides, if I really had a rich uncle, my life would be so different." This surprises me.

"Really? How so?" I ask. I thought my nerdy friend was born and bred specifically to interpret weather patterns across the United States.

"Well, I probably would've been home schooled and would've hated it. Or worse, had to attend private school and would've gotten kicked out." This is true and believable. "And I would've eventually moved with my aunt and uncle to Italy where I would have fallen in love." We sigh at exactly the same time and laugh.

"All that does sound great, but unfortunately you don't have a rich uncle who can give us the money we need. I'm going to crawl in the back and make some calls. You're on your own." I unlatch myself and crawl to the back. Maddox is happy to have a traveling buddy again. He shoves his head into my side for a quick hug and I end up giving him a few minutes of a much needed loving session.

After about two hours of getting absolutely nowhere on the phone or via e-mail, I stretch out and wrack my brain again trying to come up with a way out of this awful mess. I'm going to have to hit up all the big companies who already support or sponsor the university in some fashion. Weather is big for us since we're located in an active area. Plus, a lot of big companies are located in the Midwest so there's hope. I draft a serious letter and create a spreadsheet of companies who've been known to give money for all sorts of efforts. I just hope that all the amateurs out on the road haven't ruined this opportunity, too.

"Okay, we need to find a library or work station. I need to spread out," I say. Hunter pulls over and we review our options for the next twenty-four hours. I need space and she needs a low pressure front. She studies Doppler and NOAA and tries to put us near the closest one.

"How about we continue driving north and stay somewhere near Topeka? That way we're close enough to the action, and Topeka has all the amenities you'll need. What are you thinking anyway?" I explain to her my idea of hitting up the larger private companies. I want to do some research on which ones have had tornado damage in the past. That isn't the way I want to do it, but desperate times call for desperate measures. I decide to include Dr. Williams in my plan in case we're doubling our efforts.

"Have you heard from Kate today?" Hunter asks. Now that I think about it, I haven't. I frown.

"No. I wonder what's going on? There's nothing around us for miles. Maybe they are headed up to Nebraska. That front will bring weather up there, too. I'll shoot her a message." I reach for my phone and type a friendly hello to her.

Hi. I was just thinking about you.

That makes me smile. I can't wait to see her again.

Hopefully good things.

Nothing but!

I'm still smiling. God, I miss her. I miss the way she smells and how she hovered from the back seat to the front, Maddox's head resting on her lap. I miss her quiet nature in public and her assertiveness behind closed doors. I need to touch her and taste her again. There is no way I'm going to be able to wait until the chasing season is over.

Where are you now? Anywhere close to Topeka?

That's where we're staying tonight. Are you going to be there, too?

Yes. I need to work for a bit so Hunter is finding us a place for the night.

Send me the hotel information. Maybe we can be close.

I love that she says it that way. I will find her. Topeka isn't that big. I keep my response casual so I don't appear desperate.

Will do.

I throw in a happy face because I'm happy and I'm excited to see her again.

"So what's going on? What's that enormous grin for?" Hunter asks. We make eye contact in the rear view mirror and she winks at me.

"Kate says they are going to be in Topeka tonight, too. I'm supposed to let her know where we are staying. Maybe we can meet them for dinner or something."

"Or something," Hunter says. "Well, if they aren't staying in the same hotel, then you can have the SUV and find her. Anything for true love."

I roll my eyes at her. "Let me get to know her first, okay?" My blood is racing. I get to see Kate. She's only got a few more days before she has to be back at OSU and then I won't see her for sure until I'm done. Unless a massive storm hits Stillwater, which I hope doesn't happen.

"I'd say you know her pretty well," Hunter says. Physically, yes. Emotionally, not at all. She's still very private and I'd like to know more about her family life. Something happened to make her so shut off about them. I want to be the one she turns to when it or anything else bothers her.

"She's not real open with her life, though. I mean, I don't know the simple things. Like what's her favorite color or what she wears on the weekends. Does she work out? Where does she live? In an apartment, a house, a condo? There's just so much I don't know." I wonder if I should have asked her more questions. I didn't want to seem invasive, but maybe I missed my opportunity.

"That's what dating is all about. Yes, you guys did do things backward, but it seems to be working," Hunter says. She's right. We did start things off in the opposite direction. Most people strive to reach the point of sex. I'm straining just for conversation.

CHAPTER FOURTEEN

Thankfully, Topeka isn't expensive. We find a relatively cheap, but clean hotel and I head down to the office center to organize. I'm the only one there so I spread out my notes on the conference room table and begin my project. I text Kate to let her know where we're staying and ask her if they would be interested in dinner again. I check my e-mail and read rejection letter after rejection letter. Sigh. Dr. Williams tells me he likes my idea of trying to hit the larger corporations and tells me to go for it. Basically, that means he's not going to do anything else and it's all up to me. My mess, my problem. I rub my eyes and look at my phone again. It's almost six thirty and no word from Kate or Hunter. Well, Hunter is probably asleep and I don't know about Kate. I'm rubbing a kink out of my neck when I hear a familiar voice behind me.

"Do you need some help with that?" Her low voice gives me chills instantly. I turn to find Kate leaning against the wall watching me. She is wearing a sleeveless blouse and a skirt. I don't understand her storm chasing outfits, but she looks so damn good that I don't even tease her. I look her up and down, devouring her.

"Mmm. Sounds nice," I say. We pause for a few moments, both of us getting used to one another again. I stand up and walk over to her. "Hi."

She smiles at me. "Hi, yourself." She looks around and gives me a hug. I manage to refrain from moaning when our bodies touch. "Are you ready for a break? Do you want to grab dinner?"

"I need a shower and I need to check on Maddox. Are you staying here?" I ask. She nods. Thank God. I know for a fact she isn't sharing a room with Gage so if the offer is there, we will have some privacy tonight. I'll save my happy dance for when I'm alone. I can't let her know she affects me this much. I'm older so I should act it.

"Do you need help cleaning up?" For a moment, I think she's talking about showering with me, but her eyes are on the mess on the conference table.

"No, thank you." I scoop the piles up and close the laptop. I realize my hair is pulled back in a tiny tail so I nonchalantly let my hair down. It swoops down into my face. I still when I feel Kate's fingers in it, tucking the side behind my ear.

"I love your hair. It's so thick and dark," she says. She's very close to me again. Her fingertips find the back of my neck and start lightly scratching. Christ, that feels amazing. I close my eyes and roll my head back against her fingertips. She surprises me by leaning forward and kissing my neck. "Mmm. Why are you always so warm?" I keep my head tilted back because her lips feel amazing. I know we're one closed door away from another hot and heavy make out moment, but I'm sure the hotel has security cameras in here. I take a half step back from her.

"There isn't much privacy here, Kate," I say. She smiles at me. She knows this and doesn't care. Her eyes look so blue and I can't help but just stare at her. I reach out and run my fingertips across her cheek and down to her very red and full lips. "I miss your mouth against mine."

"Then why are you backing away from me?" So many inappropriate things pop into my head, none I can share with her just yet.

"Because I know for a fact that once we start, we won't stop." I take another step back.

"Start what?" She's teasing me, moving closer. Perhaps now would be a good time to teach her a lesson. I stop moving and she is right up against me again. She pulls on my shirt and I surprise her by lifting her up and setting her on the conference room table. I stand between her legs and pull her closer to me. I'm curious if she's wearing underwear right now. I move my face closer to hers. I watch her reaction as I snake my hand under her skirt. They widen with surprise and her right eyebrow arches. Her thighs feel like silk and I remember how they shook around me the last time she came. I find lace under the skirt. Her mouth opens slightly and her nostrils flare. She hasn't broken eye contact with me. A slight blush creeps up her neck and spreads across her cheeks. I find the transformation fascinating. I've never taken the time to watch somebody become aroused. Goosebumps cover her arms and I can see the faint outline of her nipples straining against the lace of her bra. I want to skip dinner and make love to her. We aren't going to make it to the room. I lean close so that my lips are almost touching hers. I dart my tongue out and barely touch her upper lip. She makes a noise that sounds like regret when I pull away. I move slowly back to her and nip at her bottom lip. Her hands are grabbing the table, her knuckles white against the dark wood.

"What are you hungry for, Kate?" I ask. My other hand finds its way up her skirt, both palms now tight against her thighs. If I slide my fingers a few inches, I know I'm going to find her pussy wet and swollen with need.

"You, Tristan." Her honesty is refreshing and almost brings me to my knees. I move away from her and reach my hand out to her.

"Then let's get out of here." I shove all my paperwork into my bag, grab my laptop, grab Kate's hand, and we leave. "Where are you?" I ask. She points down the hall. I'm glad it's not on the second or third floor. We'd never survive the elevator ride. As we walk to her room, I start worrying that she thinks I'm in this only for the sex. She seems as much into it as I am, so I remind myself to settle the fuck down and just go with it.

"Here, Tris." She stops and pulls out her card.

I'm patient. I have decided to be patient. I curb the part of me that wants to take the card from her hand and try to unlock the door myself because she isn't having any luck. Instead, I lean against the door and watch her. Her brow is furrowed in frustration and she's biting her bottom lip. She turns to me, card in hand. Before she says anything to me, she leans over and delivers a kiss that leaves me shaking.

"Help, please?"

I take the card from her. "Is this the right room?" We both look at the number on the door.

"Yes, this is it." She sounds frustrated. I turn her toward me and rub her arms.

"Let's try again." I gently place the card in the slot and the door clicks to green. Cards are convenient, but keys are a sure thing.

"Thank you," she says. I push the door open and she walks by me, grabbing my hand and pulling me in. I don't hesitate to follow. When we hear the click of the door locking, she turns and is immediately in my arms, fighting to take off my clothes. Her nails are scratching me, but I don't even care. I accidentally pop a few of the buttons off her blouse in my haste, but she doesn't seem to mind either. I don't even bother with the skirt. I pull it up with one hand and tear off her panties with the other. One day we will make slow, sweet love, but not today. My body is pulsing everywhere, my heartbeat almost frantic. I'm desperate to feel her skin against mine again.

"I've missed you," I say.

She stops for a moment and gives me a heart-stopping smile. "It's been dull without you."

Okay, so it's not what I wanted to hear exactly, but I'll take it. We start kissing again and I lean forward until she falls back onto the bed. Amazing body. I'm ashamed at my roughness. I lean down and kiss her stomach while my hands find the zipper on the side of her skirt and unzip her. She is panting, her body rising against my lips and falling down with each exhale. She takes off her thin, lacy bra and is finally naked beneath me. I love that her body is smooth and perfect. She smells like strawberries and sex.

I lower my head and start a trail of kisses from her collarbone all the way down to the junction of her thighs. She is wet and eager for me. The closer my mouth gets to her core, the higher her hips lift off of the bed to reach me. She moans and hisses loudly when I enter her. She feels tight and warm and I wait for her to adjust to me. I gently suck her clit and start moving my fingers in and out of her. I'm moving slowly on purpose. Every gasp, every moan, every slight buck of her hips I feel physically and now emotionally. I'm becoming far too attached to this woman. She tightens her grip on my shoulders and her legs start closing around me. She is close. I move deeply inside of her until I feel her release surround me. I drown myself in her orgasm, riding the waves with her, marveling at the way she embraces it. Not too many women are as open as Kate. I lay my head on her thigh until her breathing returns to normal. I'm about to get up when I feel her fingers twirling my hair. Maybe I can wait a few more minutes.

"I'm going to check on Maddox and Hunter. Then we can grab something to eat if you want," I say. I look up at her and am surprised by the sad look on her face. She tries to cover it up, but it's too late. "Hey, are you okay?" I slide up her body and rest beside her, drawing her close to me. "Did I do something wrong?" She smiles and waves like it's nothing, but not before I see a tear slide down her face. I feel like a jerk right now. I don't know what to do to help her because I don't know her like I should. All I can do is hold her. Everybody needs to be held from time to time. I wait until she is ready to talk. I stroke her long hair, playing with the waves, watching them cascade through my fingers. I tell her about a few funny things that happened to us yesterday. Finally, she smiles. She looks at me, but this time her eyes are bright and the sadness is gone. She brings my hand up and puts her palm against mine. Her fingers are slender and pale.

"We can always order room service," she says. I look around and laugh.

"This hotel doesn't have room service, doll. Maybe they serve some snacks down in the bar, but if we want food, we'll have to leave this room," I say. She pouts. I kiss her. "Or I could bring us back something." That makes her smile. "Okay, let me go check on everybody and then I'll bring us back nourishment in the form of greasy, fattening food."

"Or a salad," she says. I laugh.

"Or a salad," I say. I find my T-shirt and throw it back on. I really don't want to leave her, but I think she's better now and I do have to get some things done. "I'll be back in an hour, okay?" She nods at me, the sheet covering her body. I lean down and kiss her firmly again. "Call me if you need anything else." I gather up my stuff, look at her one last time and head out. I have no idea what just happened in there. Even the really great sex is confusing to me now. Something is eating her up inside and I don't know what it is or how to help her.

❖

"Did Kate find you?" Hunter asks when I walk into the room. Maddox greets me with a hug and a kiss. I rub his ears and tell him to get his leash.

"Yeah, she found me in the office downstairs. I'm going to get us dinner and head to her room, if you don't mind. I can even take Maddox with me." I'm feeling guilty at abandoning my road family.

"Don't worry about it. Time apart is good for us. Me and the boy need to bond," she says. "Do you want me to pick you up some food, too?" I ask. She nods happily. "Let me take him out for a bit and then I'll be back to grab a quick shower." I grab Maddox and we head out for a quick walk. We stop at the restaurant across the parking lot and I slip in to place an order to go. Maddox patiently waits outside. He's anxious to go for a run and the empty field across the street is perfect for him to expel his energy. I let him off his leash and he takes off at full speed. He's so happy. I keep looking at my watch. It's been thirty minutes since I left Kate and I have an incredible desire to be back with her. I cut Maddox's time short and he reluctantly returns to my side. We grab the food and I head back to the hotel. I have fifteen minutes. I give Hunter her food and jump in the shower. This time I shave. Everywhere. I now have two minutes to get downstairs.

"Don't worry about us. We'll see you in the morning," she says. How she can talk coherently with a mouth full of fries is impressive. I grab the food and head downstairs. Kate answers the door immediately.

"You are late. By one minute," she teases. She pulls me inside. She looks at my yoga pants and T-shirt. "Comfy?"

I nod. "And most importantly, clean." She laughs. Even though she's dressed comfortably, she still looks refined and polished. I hold up the bag of food and she claps with delight. She's adorable when she smiles. I melt a little.

"Let's have dinner in bed," she says. She's definitely in a much better place mentally than she was an hour ago. We pull back the covers and I prop up pillows and point for her to sit. She does and I hand her a salad. I have a sandwich and chips.

"It's a good thing I know you a little bit because deciding on dinner wasn't hard." I'm proud of myself as I watch her devour her salad.

"You know a lot about me," she says.

I can't help but laugh. "I don't know about that, but I'd like to give it a try," I say. She stares at me for a long time and I wonder if I have something on my face.

"You know what I like to eat, the music I like, what I do for a living for now, my favorite clothes. You probably know me better than anybody else, Tristan." That surprises me. I decide to try to lighten the mood.

"Tell me about your best friend back in Stillwater," I say. "You know my two best friends already. Hunter and Maddox. I couldn't imagine life without them." She smiles when I mention their names.

"I really don't have much of a life." I wait for her to elaborate. She puts down her fork. "But I guess if I had to pick, my closest friend is probably Gail. She lives in my building. She's older and is very much like a mother figure. She's super sweet and is constantly baking for me. At school, I keep to myself for the most part. Sometimes my brother and I hang out, but he's got frat life going on so it's not as much as I would like. I talk to Gage and a few others, but I'm not close enough to them to call them friends." She picks the fork back up, but doesn't take another bite.

I'm in disbelief. Sitting in front of me is a beautiful, smart woman who is simply fantastic and very few people know this. Whatever happened to Kate, it was bad enough that she walked away from every single person in her life before OSU.

"Well, I am thankful I got to know you. And not just because of..." I wave my hand back and forth between us. "Not just because of this. I think you're a lot of fun and you're very sweet. Maddox loves you and I go by his judgment."

"I have a lot of baggage, Tris. But I'm working through it because it's nice to have somebody like you in my life again." She smiles and leans forward to kiss me. It's a gentle and smooth kiss. More of a promising kiss than a passionate one. I'm giddy, but I keep it together because I have to maintain some level of calm or I'll freak her out. Nobody likes clingy.

"Well, you know pretty much all of my demons. The only thing that's on my plate is coming up with money for next season. God, Kate, I don't know what I'm going to do if Hunter has to go elsewhere. I need her close by," I say. I run my hands through my hair and exhale heavily.

"Is there anything she can do for the department before the chasing season?" she asks.

"I honestly don't know. We joke about a rich uncle showing up, but I really don't know what she's going to do if I can't come up with something. The other teams are important, too, but Hunter is my responsibility and I failed us both." I know I sound whiny and tonight isn't supposed to be about my problems. Tonight is supposed to be about us getting to know each other better. So far, she's opened up nicely and I feel more confident about us already. "I'll just have to keep plugging along and see what happens. I might even play the lottery."

She smiles at me. I could just sit here all night and look at her. Her hair is pulled back in a long ponytail and she is wearing leggings and a lightweight long sleeved cotton shirt. She has on entirely too many clothes.

"Are you done?" I ask her. She nods and I rid the bed of our impromptu picnic. I can feel her watching me as I move around. She's not shy about staring. That's something I'm going to have to get used to. I head back over to her, but this time I lie flat on the bed. I need to stretch. Before I have a chance to roll and face her, she pounces on me. Her playfulness tugs at my heart and I hold her close to me. "You saw how much I ate, right?" She nods. "And yet you are willing to lie on top of me." She leans up.

"Deal with it," she says and kisses me. Dealt. I hold her close as her body molds into mine. Our curves match. Her breasts press gently into mine. I could get used to this.

"Let your hair down," I say. She leans up and pulls the tie out. We're instantly cloaked by her soft hair. It's a small, private world for just us. I cup her face with both hands and bring her down slowly to my mouth. This is a different kiss. This one is full of promises. She welcomes my gentleness and slows her movements. She leans up to slip off her shirt. I slide my hands up to cup her beautiful breasts, their heaviness fill my hands. She closes her eyes and I hear her moan slightly with each touch. Her nipples are hard against my palms. I'm anxious to taste her again. I pull her down to me until I can raise up enough to bring one to my mouth.

She gasps. "Your mouth is so warm." She starts moving her hips and I still them with my hands. I need to show her that it's okay to enjoy the feeling of touch without needing to orgasm immediately. She stops and relaxes in my arms. I move my mouth to her other nipple, and I feel her hands working their way through my hair to rest on my neck. I know she wants to pull me closer to her. I can almost feel her frustration. I run my hand between the valley of her breasts down to her stomach and back up again, my fingertips drawing an imaginary path. Chills break out across her skin and the nipple inside of my mouth hardens even more. I bite it slightly and her nails dig into my neck. She rolls her head back, giving me better access to her. I wish it could be like this always. I move my hands down to her thighs. I can feel their warmth on either side of my hips. I can feel that she is already wet for me. I cup her gently and watch as she slowly rocks against my hands. I love that she knows exactly what she wants and how to get it. She opens her eyes and stares at me. The look is raw and filled with appreciation. We keep eye contact and I rub my thumb along her slit. I apply slight pressure on her clit and her eyes widen with desire.

"Take these off, Kate," I say. She climbs off of me and strips, her fingers shaking with need.

"Please, take off your clothes, too." She reaches out her hand to me and I climb out of bed and take off my clothes. I've always been shy around previous lovers, but not with Kate. The lights are on and she can see all of me and I don't even care. I know she likes my body and what I can do to hers and that's all the confidence I need. She leans over and runs her tongue along my shoulder blade. I love that tingling feeling. Her wet tongue only promises more pleasure later. I pull her to me and we continue kissing. She breaks away and gently pushes me back down on the bed. She straddles me again, like before, only this time we are both free to touch wherever we want. I automatically slide my hands up her thighs while she reaches down and gently touches my breasts. She slides her body down mine, her thighs no longer within reach. I frown and she smiles at me. "We have all night." Reaching over to the nightstand, she grabs her hair tie and pulls her hair back. I frown again. I like her hair surrounding me. She kisses me and slowly works her mouth all over my body, stopping only to nip and lick key areas that make me gasp and moan. When she reaches my pussy she runs her fingertips up and down, then gently slides two fingers inside of me. My hips lift to greet her soft thrusts, the feeling so incredible that I close my eyes and let my body just enjoy her touch. I know she is watching me. When her tongue touches my clit, I gasp at the warm, wet contact. Her mouth devours me while her fingers continue to stroke me closer and closer to the brink. I want to be greedy so I stretch it out as long as I can because I don't know when I will see her again after tonight. I manage to prolong my orgasm for only about a minute before

I give up and ride it out, wave after wave of pleasure engulfing my entire body. I feel spent and raw.

"Come here, Kate. I need you," I say. She is right next to me in an instant.

"You're beautiful when you come," she says.

I look at her and know she is dead serious. I smile gingerly at her and push my hair out of my face so that I can see her better. Her blue eyes are round with admiration, her cheeks flushed from passion. She licks her lips and I lean up and kiss them. They are so soft and full and smooth. She lays her head down on my shoulder. I can feel her heartbeat against my chest, her warmth against my skin. She is my Heaven. Shit, I'm falling for her. And it's only been a few weeks. I bring my hand up to my forehead at that realization.

"What's wrong?" Kate asks.

"I just remembered something I have to do…tomorrow," I mumble. We're nowhere near ready to share feelings. Plus, I need to figure out if I'm feeling this way because I just had an amazing orgasm or if it's something deeper.

"Right now? You think of something right now?" she asks. Okay, so maybe that wasn't the right thing to do or say. I give her a quick squeeze of an apology.

"I'm sorry, doll. I really am. You'll find out that my thoughts are scattered all over the place. What just happened here was incredible. You're incredible." I feel her relax a little in my arms. I look at the clock. It's still early. Plenty of time before we have to get up in the morning. Hours for me to apologize all up and down her body. Tonight, neither one of us will get much sleep.

CHAPTER FIFTEEN

I don't want to get up," Kate says. Her voice is thick with sleep. She's definitely not a morning person, which is why I waited as long as possible to wake her up.

"We're supposed to meet Gage and Hunter downstairs in a half an hour," I say. I lean down and lightly touch her cheek until she politely moves it.

"You didn't seem to mind my touch a few short hours ago."

She cracks an eye at me. A slow smile spreads across her face. "That was different." She closes her eyes again and snuggles down into the covers.

"I'm going to leave soon," I say. "I'm hungry."

"You would leave this sanctuary of warmth and covers for food?" She asks. I hear her yawn and groan at the same time.

"You know how I like to eat," I say. She smiles at me. Yeah, I walked into that one. "I mean, they have a waffle iron downstairs. A waffle iron," I say. Maybe repeating that will get her moving. "And syrup and butter. Oh. And fruit." I throw that last one in because I know she cares more about that than waffles.

"Okay, okay. I'm up, I'm up," she says. She flings the covers back and drags herself into the bathroom. I sit on the bed, check my e-mail, and write my mom a quick note. Within fifteen minutes, Kate comes out of the bathroom completely ready to go. Her hair is braided back and over one shoulder, which leaves a small wet mark on the front of her blouse. She looks beautiful and serious. She stares at me for about three seconds. "Are you ready? I could use a cup of coffee." I jump up, kiss her soundly, and head for the door. She's still a little sluggish, but she follows me out.

Hunter nods to me to get my attention when we walk into the dining area. Her plate is already piled high with waffles. I look at my watch.

"We're even early and you couldn't wait?" I ask. She smiles at me, a tiny piece of waffle escaping her closed lips. I laugh as she tries to suck it back in.

"Av couldn't waif," she mumbles around a mouthful of food.

"You couldn't wait? Like two whole minutes?" I ask. I shake my head at her and head for the waffle iron with Kate right behind me. We get our breakfasts. Mine consists of a syrup soaked waffle with scrambled eggs, sausage, and toast. Kate's is the predictable yogurt, fruit, and dry toast breakfast. We sit down in the empty seats and jump into Hunter and Gage's conversation.

"Well, next year it will be different. We spent so much money on the chaser car that there wasn't anything really left over. And, thanks to Kate, we're going to be able to fund more teams and get updated equipment. It's an exciting time," Gage says. "This has been a very active season already. Just in the time I've been gone, Kate has seen a handful of tornadoes. Global warming, I'm sure."

"It's been pretty crazy so far and we already have so much video and data gathered. I'll keep us busy this summer recording and understanding all of it," I say.

"I don't even know if I get to help," Hunter says.

"What do you mean?" Gage asks.

"Well, we didn't get our grant this year so next year is still up in the air. I'm going to talk to Williams to see if I can somehow work during the summer. Hopefully by then, Tris will have something figured out."

"Why don't you just apply for other grants? There has to be a ton out there, right?" Gage asks.

"Most of them are already issued. I'm about ready to hit the private sector and see if some of the larger companies who headquarter in and around Oklahoma are willing to hand out some funds," I say.

"I don't see why they wouldn't help. They're just as affected as everybody else when storms hit," Hunter says.

"Kate got us the MWSE grant. I didn't even know you could actually get government grants, really. The department head worked on the finances. I just spend what they give us," Gage says. I know he's still talking, but I've tuned him out. I can hear pounding in my ears. I stand up, my chair scraping the floor behind me, drawing even more attention to myself.

"You got the MWSE grant? You got the grant and didn't say anything to us?" I ask Kate. I stare at her. My face is so hot, I know it must be red. Kate's face turns white and she looks away. I can feel my heart hammering in my chest, the loudness inside deafening. My hands shake and I grab my backpack off of the back of my chair to have something to clench before I start throwing shit. Hunter stands in front of me, as if to run interference in case I explode.

"Yeah, why? Oh, my God. Was that the grant you were expecting?" Gage asks. He looks just as shocked as he sounds. I turn from everybody and walk away. Hunter is close on my heels.

"What the hell?" Hunter says. "It's not his fault. It's not their fault, Tris. You can't be mad at them." That makes me stop. I turn to Hunter.

"I get that it's available for anyone who does what we do and, yes, I should have tried harder, but Kate knew this whole time. She watched us agonize over it when she was chasing with us. She knew before, during, and after we had sex. Don't you think that's pretty important to share with someone you're close with?" I'm so mad at Kate right now. I see her walking toward us. I can't get back to the room without walking past her so I turn and walk out the front door of the hotel. Fresh air will help me. I need to think. I walk across the parking lot, headed nowhere in particular.

"Wait!" Kate calls from behind me. I stop out of habit, not out of need. I really need to cool off right now, not be confronted. "Just stop, Tris. Let's talk about this." This should be interesting. I face her. She walks until she is almost in my space.

"That grant was out there, I found it, and I got it. I didn't steal it from you. I'm sorry you feel that way."

"You think I'm mad because you got the grant and I didn't?" I take a step toward her. She doesn't even flinch at my closeness. "I'm mad because you've known all this time that we were waiting to hear back about the grant, stressing every day over e-mails and phone calls while you sat in the car with us knowing that we weren't going to get it."

"I didn't know how to bring it up or even if I was allowed to. I'm so new to this, I don't know the right procedure for anything. I'm sorry I hurt your feelings, I really am. I just have a hard time opening up and you were so easy to get to know. I didn't want to ruin what we've started here so I didn't say anything to you and Hunter." Her reasoning stinks.

"Professional courtesy, Kate. That's what it's called. Not that I expect a big thank you, but we took you in when your only other option was to go home. We're a community. Chasers have respect for one another." I don't remember the last time I was ever this pissed off. "And you could have said something before we had sex and I became emotionally invested in this relationship." I move in even closer to her. I can smell her hair and I hate that a part of me wants to hold her. "I feel so used right now. You got everything. The grant, the sex, your way. I have absolutely nothing else to say." This time she flinches and, satisfied at her faltering, I walk away.

CHAPTER SIXTEEN

All three of us are quiet in the car. Hunter is trying very hard to be understanding of my position, professionally and personally. Maddox is fast asleep in the back. I'm trying not to go ape shit over all of my bad luck. In the span of twenty minutes, I went from happiest girl in the world to pissed off bitch with no hope in sight. Hunter is just going to have to deal.

"Where are we headed?" Hunter asks. She packed the SUV in record time and we hit the road five minutes ago, breakfast forgotten. She's trying to get me involved, get my mind off of things, but I'm seeing white right now.

"I don't care. Just drive and get us out of here." I'm looking out of the window, not seeing anything. Thankfully, Hunter kind of knows the direction we should go and starts driving north. She's very quiet and I'm thankful she doesn't press me about Kate. I think the silence is worse so I flip on the radio and avoid all heartfelt songs. I'm sure Hunter is going crazy with how fast I'm changing the stations.

"How about we just listen to an audio book? I have the new Stephen King and I've been dying to hear it," she says. She hands me her phone and I plug it in. Murder and mayhem just might be the thing to settle me down. After about thirty minutes, I'm ready to talk.

"Am I totally wrong here? Was that a totally shitty thing to do or am I overreacting?" I ask. Hunter hits pause on her iPhone.

"Yes, it was a crappy thing. I know this feels like Julie all over again, but it isn't. Kate did the same research you did and for some reason, got the grant. This sounds bad, but I understand why she didn't say anything. That would have made for a very awkward ten days with us had she said something first." She holds her hands up at me after I shoot her a horrible look. "We don't know a lot about Kate and how she operates. We know she's alone and there must have been a damn good reason why she didn't share. She doesn't strike me as a woman who is straight up mean. Before you throw all of this…whatever this is…away, think about it."

I hrmpf under my breath, but she's right. I do have the right to be pissed for a while, so I wallow for another ten minutes.

"I feel used, you know?" I say. Hunter nods in understanding. "You know I don't open up to a lot of people. Not the way I did with her. I feel dirty now." She reaches over and squeezes my hand.

"Do you mind if we stop? I really need food," she says.

I laugh out loud. "We can stop. I'm not hungry though."

"Well, we'll get you a little something just in case." She knows I'll eat whatever she puts in front of me. She finds a tiny diner that looks open and we pull into the lot. We are ushered to a booth that faces the car. I can see the tips of Maddox's ears poking up from the back seat and that gives me comfort. Hunter orders for the both of us while I play with the silverware. "Okay, let's go through everything. When did she know we were talking about the MWSE grant?"

I review my memories with Kate. "I think the time we were at the park when we were all just hanging out," I say.

"Was the name of the grant even mentioned? I thought we were just talking about the grant, but didn't actually say which one it was," she says.

"Come on, Hunter. I'm pretty sure I said it. Even if I didn't, there really is only one government grant that gives us money to chase. She even told us how hard it was to get funding for the department. She could've said she got a government grant when we were talking about ours and asked us right then what the name of it was. That was the perfect time to come clean. I would have been upset, but not irate," I say. "And I probably wouldn't have slept with her."

"I'm just trying to be fair to Kate. I would hate to see you throw something good away over a technicality," she says. "This is her first time chasing so everything is new. People, procedures, equipment. Everything. We know OSU doesn't hold hands. She probably threw herself into it and came up with the golden ticket. I can't blame her for being aggressive and going for it." I smile sadly when Hunter says Kate's aggressive. Even behind closed doors she's aggressive, I silently add. "I can blame her for being an ass to you, but it's a forgivable crime, Tris. Just chill out for a bit. Let's see what happens."

The waitress brings us our food and we eat in silence. It was a good idea to stop for food. I feel better and I know Hunter does, too. Putting distance between me and Kate has helped. I feel more in control of the situation. I don't know if I can forgive her, though, regardless of what Hunter says. I'm not one to just jump into bed with people I don't know well. I'm too emotionally invested in people and I took a chance with Kate. Now, I'm flat on the ground wondering where I'm going to get the strength to pull myself up and get on with my life.

CHAPTER SEVENTEEN

I have a bad feeling about this, Hunter." I'm watching the wedge tornado swirl up ahead. Hunter slows down to give it enough room to cross in front of us. It's hard to see because it's so dark, but we can see wood and metal flying around in its debris and I say a silent prayer that everybody is safe. The aftermath of the tornado from last week is still heavy in my heart and I wonder if Gloria, the sweet, little old lady with the injured leg is fine.

"Yeah, I'm going to pull back because it's getting bigger."

"Yeah, let's pull over and wait. Doppler says it should pass right in front of us." It's nice that neither one of us has a death wish. Hunter pulls off onto a gravel driveway and we wait the tornado out and pray it doesn't decide to change its course and head our way. About ten seconds later, Gage and Kate zoom by in Frankenstein and we both start yelling at them as if they can hear us.

"Hunter, he's going to kill them. We've got to stop him," I say. Hunter reaches for the CB microphone before I can and signals Gage.

"Gage, you are about to engage the tornado. You need to turn around," she says. We hear some static, but finally his voice comes through the radio.

"It's fine. Going to turn. Out."

"Get out of there, Gage. This doesn't look good." Hunter is trying to sound calm, but I can always tell when she's nervous and that's when I start to lose it, too. I grab the microphone from Hunter's grip.

"Gage, get the hell out of there! You're responsible for yourself and someone else." I can't bring myself to say her name out loud yet, but my meaning is clear. "The tornado is crossing right in front of us and you're headed directly into its path." Static is my only answer. I throw the microphone down in frustration.

"Get Kate on the phone," Hunter says. I reach for my phone and dial her. It rings and rings, but no answer. I get her voice mail. Shit. There is nothing we can do now except watch helplessly.

"What a total asshole." I'm so upset with Gage. I can only hold the sides of my head and cry, watching everything unfold in front of us.

"We can try to get closer," Hunter says. I shake my head because the whole thing will be over in less than a minute. The longest minute of my life. We watch the fury of wind pick up speed and cross about a quarter of a mile ahead of us. I almost throw up when I see a gray object tossed up and over as it passes the road.

"Fuck, Hunter, that's them. We got to help them!" I know I sound hysterical, but for once, Hunter doesn't scold me. She throws the SUV into gear and guns it. By the time we reach the spot where the tornado crossed the road, it's already through the field. I don't see their truck. I'm in full out panic mode. I grab my backpack and my flashlight. It's still dark from the storm and raining intensely, but I feel nothing. I need to find them. I need to find Kate. Hunter turns her flashers on and points the car in the direction where we think the truck rolled, hoping the headlights will help us see. She races over to me and we take off across the field.

"Over there, Tris." She points the flashlight to where the shaft of light reflects off of gray metal. My heart sinks and I almost fall to my knees. The truck is smashed completely. No, no, no. Hunter reaches the driver's side and shines her light in. I automatically race over to the passenger's side and shine my light in to find Kate. I'm greeted with Kate's head leaning against the shattered glass, a gash along the top of her forehead and by her ears. Her eyes are closed. I have to swallow the bile rising in my throat. Please be okay, I pray. I can't open the door so I yell for Hunter. I see Gage stirring so I know he is at least conscious. The storm drowns out my voice so I race around the car and grab Hunter.

"The door is stuck. I can't get it open," I yell not only because I'm panicking, but because she can't hear me over the thunder and rain surrounding us.

"Let's get Gage out, then you can crawl through this side," she says while pointing at the door. I nod in understanding. She gingerly helps Gage out. I'm about two seconds from beating the shit out of him, but Hunter gets in between me and him and looks at me. "Another time, Tris. We have more important things to do here." She sees how angry I am and I'm glad she stopped me because God only knows what I would do to him if I got my hands on him. "Go in there and see if you can get Kate to wake up." She sits Gage down on the ground and covers him with a raincoat she finds inside. I crawl in and do my best to wake up Kate without moving her.

"Kate. Kate. Can you hear me?" Her face is covered in blood and I don't know where it's coming from. Thankfully, I can see that she is breathing so I know she's still alive. "Kate, if you can hear me, say something or move your finger or something." The desperation in my voice sounds foreign to me. Hunter peeks in.

"What's going on?" she asks. The look on my face sums it up for her. "I'm dialing 9-1-1." I check the base of the radio and flip it to the emergency station. I call in our coordinates to the best of my recollection. Hunter yells that the EMTs are on their way and that she's going to move Gage back to the SUV. He's wobbly, but fully alert now. I can barely look at him. I nod to Hunter and she slowly makes her way back the way we came.

I take a quick inventory of Kate's body. The metal is crushed against her body, but nothing has broken through the door so nothing has stabbed her. I run my hands along her body. There's a bump in her arm and she moans slightly when I touch it. I pull my hand back, my stomach twisting as my brain registers a broken bone. I focus on the good. I concentrate on the fact that she was conscious enough to moan. I reach down to run my fingertips over her hand, afraid if I try to hold it, I'll injure her further. Instead I stare at her, whisper words about our time together and touch her gently where I think it's okay. About fifteen minutes later, I hear sirens and slip out of the truck to flag down the EMTs. At least the torrential rain has subsided into a steady drizzle. They hustle over to us and I try to give them as much information as I can.

"Do you know her family? Do you have somebody you can call for her?" The EMT looks at me and I stare back blankly. His question finally registers.

"Her phone. I'm sure she has an emergency contact stashed in it," I say. "What hospital are you taking her to?"

"St. Francis. It's about twenty minutes from here. You can follow us there." I watch painfully as they extract Kate from the truck. I reach out several times to help, but pull my hand back when I realize that I'm of no use. Once they have her on the stretcher, I pat her down. She doesn't have her phone on her. It must still be in the car. I only have a few minutes to search for it because they are leaving as soon as they get back to the van and I definitely want to follow them. I shine my flashlight in and find it on the floor. I grab it and chase after them.

Gage is already in the ambulance and an EMT is checking him out. I still want to throttle him. I know I'm going to write to his superior about his piss poor judgment, but not before I tear into him. I watch them slip Kate inside, secure her, and take off.

"We can follow them. They're taking her to St. Francis, which is about twenty minutes away. I hope the roads are clear." I know I sound obnoxious, but I can't seem to calm down. Hunter follows the van, putting very little distance between us and them. We arrive in fifteen minutes. Hunter agrees to take care of Maddox and meet me inside. I jump out to greet the ambulance.

"Can you fill out any paperwork?" An Emergency Room nurse gives me a clipboard with forms to fill out and I'm reminded to check her phone for her emergency contact. I find her phone in my rain jacket and flick it on. It's pass code protected. Shit. Focus, Tris. I think back to when we were naked in the hotel room last and she got a message. What was her code? I try a few numbers but the phone buzzes negatively. I suddenly remember when I had to call Hunter and Kate gave me her code. I remember the numbers, but I'm not certain of the order. After a few more tries, the phone opens. The first thing I see is my name at the top of the screen with a text message that she never had the chance to send.

I'm scared. Gage is cra

And that was it. The text she never got to finish. It breaks my heart. I scroll through her contacts and am surprised by how few there are. I see her ICE contact and dial it right away. Garrison Brighten, her brother whom she has mentioned a few times.

"Hey, Katie. What's up?" I hear on the other end. I shake my head and clear my throat.

"No, this isn't Kate. My name is Tristan Stark and I'm a…a friend of Kate's. You're listed as her emergency contact. There's been an accident." I take a quick breath before I continue.

"What's happened? What's wrong with her?" He sounds genuinely concerned and I try to keep my voice calm as I explain.

"Well, she and her storm chasing partner were caught in a tornado. Their truck rolled several times. She is at St. Francis Hospital in Maryville, Missouri. I don't know how she is doing. We just arrived. I can keep you posted."

"Have you seen her? How bad is it?"

"I really don't know, but I'll call as soon as I hear."

"I'll head up there as soon as I can. Thanks for calling and letting me know."

I give him my own phone number and we hang up. I clutch Kate's phone closer to me. I can't believe this has happened. I've never known chasers to get hit so hard, so fast. Gage was an idiot. I can feel myself getting all worked up again over his stupidity. He has no respect for human life or the well-being of his protégé. And it's not as if she was going to be with him the entire time. She only got a few weeks off and now she's going to miss even more.

"How's it going?" Hunter walks up to me and I walk into her outstretched arms. We stand there quietly for a moment. I step back and look up at her.

"I called her brother and he's on his way up here. He was pretty shook up about it." I know that I am, too, but I'm trying to be cool in front of Hunter. "How's Maddox?"

"He's fine. He ran like the devil for a bit, then settled down. I gave him his dinner and he's fat and happy in the SUV. He'll be all right for a long time." She sits us down and we wait. A doctor comes out after a half of an hour to tell us about Gage. He has a pretty bad concussion, a large goose egg on his forehead, and a sprained wrist. I'm surprised it's not worse. Hunter surprises me by asking if she can see him. The doctor agrees but only for a few minutes. She squeezes my hand and leaves. I'm still holding

Kate's phone in my other hand and unlock it. I want to read our messages. Even though it's been several days since our last texts, mine are the only ones in her phone. I hit her photo files and see photos of tornadoes, Maddox and me. There's a photo of me and Hunter in the front seat talking, a photo of me taking photos of a tornado. My heart stops when I see a photo of me asleep the last night we were together. It's actually a pretty good photo. I look peaceful and happy. Really happy. Too bad we won't get there again. Suddenly very sad, I shut her phone off and put it back in my pocket. A few minutes later, Hunter returns.

"I asked Gage if he wanted me to call Angie for him, but he said he was going to do it. He's pretty upset about everything and kept apologizing to me over and over again. He asked if we know how Kate is doing, but I told him we haven't heard yet. I doubt we will for several hours." She sits back down and stretches out beside me.

"Just so you know, I'm going to write a letter about Gage." Hunter nods.

"I understand. I would, too, if I was in your position," she says. "Just make sure to keep your emotions out of it. Or maybe I should write it since you have a relationship with Kate."

"I don't have a relationship with Kate. At least not anymore." I'm grumbling. She just looks at me. "We can both write a note since we were both present." She nods again in agreement. I'm so tired. Now that we're sitting down and my adrenaline rush is gone, I'm having a hard time keeping my eyes open.

"Tris. Tris. C'mon." Somebody is shaking me and I don't want to wake up. "The doctor is here to tell us about Kate." My eyes fly open and I'm instantly awake.

"What's going on? Can we see her?"

"I was just telling the doctor that you're her sister and were in the car behind her when the tornado hit." Really? Hunter thinks Kate and I can pass for sisters? I'm a quarter Native American and Kate couldn't be more Irish if she tried. The doctor stares at us for just a moment.

"Well, her body has been through quite a bit. She has a badly ruptured spleen that we are removing right now, a broken arm, a dislocated shoulder, a few broken ribs, and several lacerations on her face from the impact of the airbag and the window. It will be quite a while before she's out of surgery, but I wanted to let you know how she is doing. We will let you know when you can see your sister." I look away when he says that. We both know that I'm not Kate's sister.

"How long will that be?" I ask.

"Not for at least an hour or two." I nod like that's okay even though I want to go see her now. I look down at my watch and am surprised that I slept for almost two hours

"I need to call Garrison. He will want an update," I say.

Hunter nods and backs away to give me some privacy. I dial Garrison from my phone this time, but it goes straight to voice mail. I leave him a message.

"Want to go get something to eat in the cafeteria?" Hunter asks after I put my phone away. I start to shake my head, but she pulls me up out of my seat and directs me toward the cafeteria. Food is a good idea. Maybe I can stop shaking if I eat dinner.

"Let's be quick, okay? I want to be here when the doctor comes out for us to see Kate. And what's with you telling him we're sisters? Anyone can look at us and tell that we aren't related."

"I knew there was only one way to get you in there to see her. Sorry. I know it doesn't make sense, but it worked, right?" She's got a point. We grab a hot plate of mashed potatoes and gravy with meatloaf and broccoli. I don't think I can eat anything right now, but I surprise myself and Hunter by cleaning my plate and doing it before she finishes hers. That never happens.

"I wonder if Kate is going to remember anything. With that much blunt trauma…" Hunter starts. I hold up my hand to stop her.

"Don't even say it, Hunter. We won't know anything until she wakes up." I wring my napkin between my hands until Hunter reaches over to still me.

"I'm sure she will be fine, Tris. I'm sorry I brought it up." I'm sorry she did, too. I never thought that she might lose her memory or have brain damage. Now I'm a total basket case.

We are back upstairs within thirty minutes. I'm more alert and borderline anxious. We sit back down and wait. Her doctor finds us almost an hour later and tells me I'm allowed to see her. I swallow hard, trying to rid the lump that has settled in my throat as I'm led back to a row of beds separated by only sheet curtains.

"We're going to move her to her own room here in a bit, but I'm sure you want to see her right away." The doctor pulls back the curtain and my knees threaten to give out. I reach out and grab her hand before I even sit down. The blood is wiped clean, but the bruising has settled in. She looks swollen and pitiful.

"I'm here, Kate. I'm here." I don't know what else to say. I don't know where I can touch her, so I continue to squeeze her hand. She has a long road to recovery ahead of her and I feel sick. I grit my teeth and try hard to remain seated. It wouldn't be good to go on a quest to find Gage and beat the shit out of him. I can't believe how stupid he was. Even rookies know not to drive into a tornado. I have no idea what he was thinking, but I will do everything in my power to make sure that he doesn't do it again. Kate could have died. Thankfully, her seat belt saved her. I'm starting to shake again, from anger and from relief. I calm down because I don't want her to pick up on my negative energy so I take a deep breath. I gently stroke her fingers, focusing on their softness. I remember her touch against my skin and smile sadly. I don't know that we'll have that again.

"Okay, we are going to move her to her own room now." A nurse scares me as she pulls back the curtain.

"That's pretty fast," I say. I know they're busy from other injuries from the tornado and daily emergencies. She grabs another nurse and they prep Kate to move her. I'm hovering like a mother hen, hissing when they carelessly bump her against the wall, reaching out, then pulling my arm back. "Careful." They both just look at me. The elevator ride is uncomfortably quiet. After she is settled and they leave, I pull a chair close to her bed and continue holding her hand. She looks so small and helpless. Her vitals are strong, though, and I just tell myself over and over that she is going to be okay.

"That was probably an F3 tornado." I don't know what else to talk about. "You rolled about five times. The tornado just clipped Frankenstein." Maybe she doesn't want to hear about the tornado. "Maddox is worried about you." I can't quite tell her that I am, too, because I still need to process everything. "Maybe when things have settled and you're better, we can talk about things." I bring her hand up to my lips and carefully kiss the back of her hand. Exhaustion settles in and I rest my head against the side of her bed.

"Are you Tristan? Excuse me." Somebody is gently shaking me. I look up and find a tall young man who looks exactly like Kate standing about two feet away. I jerk back. I'm still holding Kate's hand.

"Yes, yes, I am," I say. I stand up to properly introduce myself to the man I assume is Garrison, Kate's baby brother. He's over six feet tall, all athlete, and drop dead gorgeous.

"I'm Gary. Thank you for calling me and letting me know about her." He looks worried. "How is she?" I sit back down, and start gently rubbing her uninjured arm.

"They had to remove her spleen. She also has three broken ribs, a broken arm, and several stitches. The doctor says she will be fine though…" I trail off because it doesn't need to be said. She looks horrible. Gary grabs another chair and pulls it up on the other side of Kate. He places his hand on her leg, giving it a quick, supportive squeeze. We're silent for about ten minutes or so. I have no idea what to say to him, but I try to strike up a conversation.

"So you're at OSU with Kate?" He nods. He looks pale and frightened. I'm amazed at how much they look alike. Same strawberry blonde hair and bright blue eyes. The door opens and another man enters the room. Gary immediately jumps up. Judging from his reaction and how similar they all look, I know I'm about to meet their dad. After quick introductions, Gary offers Ben his chair beside Kate's bed.

"Can you tell me what happened?" Ben asks. I'm reluctant to throw Gage under the bus because, even though Ben is calm and quiet, he strikes me as a man who can make or break somebody with a simple phone call. There's probably a good reason why Kate never talks about her father so I proceed with caution.

"Kate's mentor, Gage, was trying to get closer to the tornado and misjudged the direction. Their truck was clipped as he turned to get out of its path." I'm satisfied with that explanation. Ben just gives me a curt nod. He rubs his hand over his face a few times before looking straight at me. His eyes are piercing and alert even though his face is haggard and his suit crumpled. We are quiet for a few minutes before Ben engages me again.

"How do you know Katie?" I smile at his nickname for her. That's very fitting.

"Hunter and I know Gage and Kate because we work at OU. They're our friendly rivals. Kate rode with us for a little over a week while Gage was home with a family emergency."

Ben looks at me for more information and I really don't know what else to tell him. I'm certainly not going to tell him about us. If he doesn't know who Gage is, then he sure as hell won't know who I am. "We saw about three tornadoes during that time and captured some incredible video and data. Safely." He nods.

"Is Gage known for being a cowboy?" He asks. This is where it gets sticky. I don't know what Kate will say so I need to be careful. Based on the text that never got sent to me, I don't think she will care what I say, but I don't want to ruin her chances at progression within her department. I keep it as politically correct as I can.

"He is kind of a daredevil, but I know that this experience really shook him up," I say.

"He's still here?" Ben asks. He sits up straighter and his eyes narrow with anger. I let go of Kate's hand for the first time since we got into this room so that I can reach out and squeeze Ben's hand briefly.

"He is, but there is a time and a place and now isn't it." I silently add, get in line, because I get first dibs at him. He nods in agreement and we lean back and relax for the first time.

"Can I get you a cup of coffee or anything?" I ask.

"Coffee would be great, thank you."

"Gary? Would you like some coffee?"

"Yeah, thanks. I'm exhausted from the drive." Gary nods his thanks.

I leave Kate's side and head down the hall to the visitor's lounge. I'm surprised to see Hunter there, thumbing through an old magazine.

"Hey. How is Kate?" she asks.

I'm tempted to curl up in her lap and settle in for a long, much needed hug. Instead, I plop down in the chair next to her and sigh. "The same. Her brother and father showed up. I can understand why Kate has kept her dad a secret."

Hunter's eyes widen. "Oh, my God. What's wrong with him? Is he a criminal or something?" I can practically see the wheels of her imagination turning. I stop her before it gets out of control.

"No, he's like super business man or something. He oozes power. And he's probably had a few people killed," I say. She nudges me and we both smile. "Well, now that she has her family here, I guess we can take off. Her doctor says she should make a complete recovery." I remember the coffee for Ben and Gary. Hunter waves me off and dives back into the six-month-old magazine. I pour three cups of strong waiting room coffee, grab some sugar and creamer packets and head back down the hall.

Ben is now on the side of the bed where I was and is holding Kate's hand. It's sweet. He stands up to take the cup of coffee and move, but I motion for him to stay there. "I think she needs her dad right now. Hunter and I are going to get back on the road now that you're here. Please keep me posted on her progress. I would appreciate it." He nods and moves out of my way as I say good-bye to Kate. I hold her hand again, give it a squeeze, and whisper words I don't want her dad to hear. I don't really want her to hear them either, but I need to get them off of my chest. I can't help but place a soft kiss on her lips. I'm gentle because she has a small cut on the corner of her mouth. I smile at Ben and Gary, grab my awful coffee, and walk out of the room. The hallway is blurry as tears cloud my eyes. I make a quick stop in the bathroom before I collect Hunter and we leave.

CHAPTER EIGHTEEN

There is no place like home. I'd say it three times, but I'm already here. We were on the road until the very last week in June and probably could have continued, but all three of us were ready to be done. I have enough data to process until next season. Hunter was missing James. Even Maddox ran off into the fields doing God knows what when I stopped the car in our driveway. I had to whistle for him several times before he came back hours later. We all love home.

It's the first week of July and Hunter and James are throwing a Fourth of July party at their apartment complex. It's cute how they are together. Hunter threatened an intervention again if I didn't attend the party, so I'm here and I'm trying not to think about Kate. It's getting easier, at least that's what I'm trying to tell myself. We're all by the pool, drinking beer and listening to music. I'm not really into it, but out of respect for Hunter, I play along. My feet are in the water, enjoying the coolness on this humid Oklahoma day. There are several people from our department, as well as several women who are giving me a lot of attention. My gaydar is off the chain and I think Hunter is trying to play matchmaker today.

"Do you mind if I sit here?" A very leggy brunette points to the concrete block next to me and I smile at her.

"Have a seat." I nervously move my legs back and forth in the water. I've been out of practice too long to play it cool.

"I'm Mindy." She's tan and lovely and I couldn't care less.

"Tris."

"How do you know Hunter and James?" she asks.

"I work with Hunter at OU. How do you know them?" I ask.

"I'm James' little sister's best friend." She laughs as I process the relationship. "So do you chase tornadoes, too?"

"Yes. We actually just finished up this season."

"That's so cool. How many tornadoes did you see?" Suddenly, she sounds like a frat boy and I lose interest.

"A couple dozen or so. It was pretty active at the beginning, but pretty quiet the last six weeks."

"Probably global warming," Mindy says. Why does everybody say that?

"What is it that you do?" I know I need to pretend to engage with her. Otherwise, Hunter will be annoying later.

"I'm a reporter for Channel 14 news. Just on the weekends, though."

"That's interesting." I'm somewhat impressed. We're quiet for a moment. I sip my beer.

"So are you dating anyone?" she asks. I shake my head no.

"What about you?" I ask just to keep the conversation going.

"My girlfriend and I are taking a break. I guess that makes her my ex-girlfriend," she says.

"How long ago?"

"It's been about three months." I nod. "It's hard being single during the summer. That's when all of the fun stuff happens." I smile at that. I couldn't care less about this party, but for fear of Hunter admitting me somewhere, I promised myself that I would show up and converse with people. Pool parties are supposed to be fun.

"Yeah, it's been a few months since my last date, too," I say.

"What happened?" she asks. "If it's not too personal." Of course it is, but I play along.

"Like most relationships, the trust factor failed," I say. She smiles sadly at me. She knows what that's like.

"Well, let's toast to having fun today and forgetting about the past. At least for one day." She tilts her beer at me and I clink it. That actually sounds like a good idea. I know that if I drink too much, Hunter will let me crash on her couch. Maddox is sitting over in the shade next to the food. I trust Hunter to take care of him, too.

"Do you have your bathing suit on?" Mindy asks. She lifts up my shirt playfully. I push her hands away.

"No, I'm not much of a swimmer."

"Well, how are we going to challenge anybody here to chicken if you don't have your bathing suit?" she says. I'm wondering if she's going to be on my shoulders or if I'm going to be on hers. She's tall, but lithe and I'm average with muscle. Hmm. Suddenly, I'm wishing I had my bikini with me.

"I'm sure Hunter has something I can borrow," I say. The idea is starting to grow on me.

"Hey, Hunter," Mindy yells. Hunter looks at us and a slow smile creeps over her face. I glare at her. She winks back. "Do you have a bathing suit for Tris here?" She points down at me like Hunter isn't going to know who I am.

"As a matter of fact, I do. C'mon, Tris." She motions me to follow her.

I hand Mindy my beer and jump up. "I'll be right back." I smile at her and try not to skip over to Hunter.

"So, what's going on over there?" she asks as we walk over to her apartment.

"Nothing. Just talking. She has your favorite job in the world," I say. She rolls her eyes at me. Apparently, she knows all about Mindy. "What's her story?"

"You know as much as I do. Pretty, single, smart. Well, sort of smart," she says. I laugh. "She's smart. I wouldn't invite anybody who wasn't. I know you."

"She's friendly. And she wants me to be her partner in chicken," I say.

"When was the last time you played chicken?" she asks.

"I'm pretty sure it was grade school." We slip into her apartment and she digs around until she finds a dark blue one piece suit that will work. I put my shorts on and we head back to the pool. Mindy is still there holding our beers.

"Did you find us any challengers?" I ask. She smiles at me. It's a nice, sweet smile.

"I wanted to make sure you would find something to wear first," she says. "Blue's a good color on you." She's looking at me appreciatively and I actually don't mind. Mindy is an attractive woman. Very attractive. Her bikini is tastefully revealing and she's not afraid to show off her body. I've decided she's going to be on my shoulders.

"I'm going to round up more beers and you're going to find us some suckers," I say. She laughs and slides into the pool. I grab a few more beers. We aren't supposed to have glass bottles near the pool so I find a few cans instead.

"We have our first victims," Mindy says. She points at James and Allison, one of the women in his band. Thankfully, James is not very scrappy so our chances are good. I put our cans down, slip off my shorts and dive in. I surface right in front of Mindy.

"Climb on," I say. I duck under and feel her legs hook over my shoulders. I ease her up and am surprised by how light she is. I hold her thighs tightly against my shoulders as she finds her balance. I can feel the heat between her legs against my neck. It's sexy.

I walk us over to our challengers and the girls start wrestling. James and I smile at each other because we both know how sexy this is. I'm holding on to Mindy and she's doing a great job of pushing Allison around until they plop backward giving us our victory. I lower Mindy into the water and she slides off of me. She hugs me as soon as I resurface. I smile and it feels good. I can't remember the last time I smiled so much. Actually I do, but I don't want to think about Kate right now.

"That was great," Mindy says. She still has her arm draped around my shoulders, the hug never quite ending. "Let's get some food to go with our beers." We climb out of the pool and grab a few plates of food. Maddox crawls out from underneath the table and Mindy screams.

"What the hell?" I say. Maddox slinks back under the table, his ears flat against his head. I reach under and pet him until he slowly crawls back out and leans up against my legs. "This is Maddox. He's my baby and completely harmless." By the look on Mindy's face, I can tell she is not convinced.

"Why is he scarred?" she asks. She looks repulsed and now I'm no longer interested.

"He had a bad puppyhood. He's very sweet and he wouldn't hurt you, I promise."

Mindy looks at us warily. "I'm going to find us a place to sit down." She backs away from us slowly.

"It's okay, boy. She just doesn't know you yet." I'm sad for Maddox. I can tell his feelings are hurt and I try to make him feel better with a quick loving session. He shakes it off and wags his tail after several kisses and cracker treats. We walk over to where Mindy is sitting.

"I'm sorry about that. I just haven't had a lot of luck with dogs. I got bit by one when I was little and I guess I haven't gotten over it," Mindy says. I understand her hesitancy and I don't push her to get to know Maddox. He curls up under my chair looking guiltily at Mindy. She does her best to ignore him.

"It's okay. He's a perfect dog, really. He's never hurt anybody before. Maddox is my best friend, other than Hunter." Mindy doesn't look amused. I don't push it. Kate was all over him the first time she met him. She trusted him and loved him the minute she saw him. She didn't scream. I sigh. Mindy isn't Kate and I shouldn't compare the two. I'm not being fair to Mindy. "Do you have any pets at all?" I ask. She shakes her head.

"I don't have time for pets. My job keeps me pretty busy and it's not fair to them. Is Maddox your only pet?" I can tell she's trying, but she's definitely not an animal lover. That's a problem.

"Yes. One day I won't be gone every spring chasing storms. I'll be home more and then I'll have more pets." She nods at me, completely not interested. Time to change the subject. "So, what do you like to do when you aren't working so hard?"

"I like to go out, have a good time with friends. It seems like I'm always on the go, really," she says. We're completely opposite. Other than physical attraction, we've got zip. Now I need to make a decision. I can walk away or have a good time tonight. I'm guessing that Mindy won't care either way. She offers to get us another beer, but I've already made my decision.

"Well, actually, I have to be somewhere else tonight, but thanks for the offer. Speaking of which…" That's my cue to leave and her cue to know that this isn't going any further.

"Thanks for being my partner today, Tristan. I had a good time," Mindy says. She smiles at me.

"It was fun. Thanks for getting me out of my funk. Have fun here. These bashes are usually pretty wild." She stands when I do and gives me another hug. It's nice feeling her body against mine, but not enough to make me stay. I wave goodbye. Maddox and I head over to Hunter.

"Are you leaving?" Hunter asks. Concern is etched on her face.

"Hey, I lasted a few hours, right? And I did have fun. I'll talk to you soon." Maddox and I climb into the Jeep and we head home. That was a lot of socializing for both of us. It was nice to get out and feel a spark with a woman again, but now I just want to snuggle with Maddox and make him feel special.

CHAPTER NINETEEN

"What're you doing?" Hunter pokes her head into my office without knocking, scaring the shit out of me. I throw a pen at her.

"Christ, why can't you knock like everybody else?" I'm already pissy.

"Chill. What's going on?" She sits down in the guest chair and acts as if I'm not in a foul mood. She's been extremely considerate toward me since we ended our season. Thankfully, she hasn't mentioned Kate since we returned.

"They finally posted the grant and I'm reading some back up. It's weird because there are several chunks missing," I say.

"Chunks?" Hunter asks.

"Yeah, like complete sections. Important sections. This all seems weird if you ask me," I say.

"Always the conspiracy theorist," Hunter says.

"I just don't like losing." But it's more than that. I don't like losing grants or my heart. "I've asked Bob Garner to send me the missing pages. They're required to make all of the backup public. He said he would look into it and get it to me sometime this week. I just don't like the way this whole thing went down."

"Have you heard anything else from any others?" Hunter asks. I've kept her in the loop on the different grants and government scholarships I've applied for and we've celebrated all the ones that have come in, from one hundred dollars to one thousand.

"Not this week, but there are still a few I'm waiting on," I say. Hunter knows it's not nearly enough for next season, but it should be enough to at least get us there. "This just sucks. I'm really sorry, Hunter."

"Stop it. What's done is done. If there's anything you need help with, I'm your girl," she says.

"Thanks, but now it's just a matter of waiting. There's nothing else out there. We have a few fall fundraisers coming up this semester, but I don't know how much that will bring in. Do you know how much I hate waiting?" She smiles at me. We both hate waiting. It's amazing we are good at our jobs. Most of the time we are driving and waiting.

❖

It takes Bob a week to send me the missing pages. I find it interesting that he's mailed them to me instead of e-mailing them. That would have been a lot quicker and easier. It's not until I read through all of the pages that I realize the reason for so much secrecy. One name stands out. I almost missed it, but I'm rather sensitive to the name at the moment and my eyes find it and hold until my brain reads all the words before and after it. Ben Brighten.

"Are you kidding me?" I say. Nobody is around to hear me, but I can't help but vocalize my disbelief. I dial Hunter.

"What up, dawg?" she asks. She's so professional.

"You need to come to my office. It's urgent. You're not going to believe what I found out." I hear the click of the phone and I know she's on her way. Drama always gets Hunter moving. She's sitting in my guest chair with the door closed within thirty seconds. I hand her the piece of paper after I highlight the name.

"No way," she says.

I nod at her. "Yep. Daddy helped get the grant."

"Nobody has that much power, do they?" Apparently, there is more to Ben Brighten than we realized. I was just kidding when I told her he's probably had people killed. Now, I'm not so sure. He at least has muscles big enough to put the squeeze on some important military people. No wonder Bob didn't want to e-mail me the pages. Somebody doesn't want this information to get out. I'm surprised nobody else has questioned it. I know that I've been e-mailed by other universities when I was awarded the grant who had tons of questions for me. Nobody has said or posted a word about this. It's all so weird.

"Well, there's one way to find out," Hunter says. I shake my head no. I'm not calling Kate. I've found peace in my miserably lonely state and so far it's working for me.

"I'm just going to work harder and prod people more to give us money, that's all." I know we are at the bottom of the barrel. Maybe I need to head out and visit people face to face. It's harder to say no when I'm right there in front of them.

"Good luck with that," Hunter says. "I still can't believe this. We should talk to Bob and ask if we can help him find his balls." She's so eloquent.

"It's probably not Bob's fault. I'm sure somebody put the squeeze on him. Bob's in our corner." I say that with not a lot of conviction. I just don't know anymore.

"Well, at least we know who we have to fight next year," Hunter says. "I don't know that we can, but at least we know." She gets up and heads out of my office. "Don't worry. I'll ask my mom to invite some of her rich, snobby friends to the fundraiser in October. Maybe one of them will write a check." She gives me an encouraging smile and leaves my office. I'm still stunned. I feel worse than I did when I first found out. That wound is open again, but this time I've pushed out most of the emotions. Most, but not all.

CHAPTER TWENTY

The first day of classes is always the worst. It's hot, the students are unsettled because they already miss summer after only one day, and I'm wearing a suit and heels. I can't remember the last time I wore makeup. Well, actually, I can but I don't want to think about it. It was that magical night in Lawrence, Kansas when Kate and I had our fantastic all night date. I frown at my memory, upset with the entire situation. I wish I could completely forget the last three months of my life. I turn to the board and write Tristan Stark, Meteorology 101. The murmurs of the students eventually quiet and I face a silent classroom. There are approximately one hundred and twenty students in this class, but I know I will lose about half of them by December. Unless you really love weather, this class tends to lean toward the boring side, especially when I'm required to follow the textbook. Whenever I see my students secretly pull out their phones to text or play games, I spice things up by showing them my videos or photos. That usually keeps their interest the rest of the class. I can't wait until I can teach the upperclassmen. Then, it seems like it will be worth it, but that won't happen for another year.

"Good morning, class. I'm Tristan Stark. Welcome to Meteorology 101. If this isn't your class, then get out." The class chuckles a bit and we settle in for the next fifty minutes. I start off with the basics. What weather is, how it affects us, why it's good, why it's bad. I try to keep it light because I don't want to lose them on the first day. I give them the first two chapters to read before the next class and excuse them a few minutes early. I breathe a sigh of relief when they rise and leave the room.

The first day is hard for me, too. I have to get used to being around people again. I spent the summer moping in my house. My only visitors were Hunter and her boyfriend. They managed to get me to go out a few times, but only because I could tell Hunter was truly worried about me and I didn't want any type of intervention. She knows how to get in touch with my family and isn't afraid to do so. The last thing I need is for my mother to visit.

"You did a good job of keeping their interest on the first day. Not too many professors can say that."

My hand falters as I reach for my papers. I know that voice. I close my eyes. I settle my heart and tuck it back into my chest where it belongs so that I don't choke on it in my throat. I don't want to turn around. I don't want to open myself up again. Steeling myself against the onslaught of emotions, I face Kate. She is even more beautiful than I remember. I stare at her until it becomes uncomfortable. At least for me. She doesn't seem affected by it. A huge part of me wants to fall into her arms and weep that she is fine. The last time I saw her, she was bruised, swollen, and broken. Even pissed at her, I still prayed that she would be okay. From the looks of it, she is okay. Her face is smooth, her arm isn't in a cast. She is lovely. Her lips are almost curved, her eyes searching my face for some sort of sign if she can smile or not. I take a deep breath before I say anything.

"What are you doing here, Kate?" I ask. I grab my bag and continue gathering up my stuff. My body is trembling and I don't want her to see me like this.

"I wanted to see how you're doing and to thank you for saving my life that day." Her voice is so sincere. I know she means it, but I'm still pissed. I know I'm being irrational at this point and probably sabotaging any chance of a relationship I could possibly have with her.

"No need to thank me. You needed my help and I'm glad we were there for you both." I emphasize the word both. "And I'm doing fine." I turn and smile. It's fake. The smile I reserve for photos. "I'm glad you're doing well. The last time I saw you, you didn't look so great." I want to get out of this room, but my body is suddenly very heavy and my heart is tired.

"Maddox and I now have matching scars," she says playfully. She tilts her head to the side, pulling her hair back to show me a scar that is fresh and pink along her hairline. My stomach churns as I remember seeing it oozing blood with her beautiful hair matted against it. "Do you have another class right now? If not, can we go somewhere and talk?"

"No. I have things to do. It's my first day and I just…can't," I say.

Her face falls and I almost feel regret. Her hair is lighter from the summer sun and she seems even thinner, but still just as beautiful. I'm itching to touch her. I clutch my bag tighter to keep myself from reaching out to her. "Thanks for letting me know you're all right." I walk around her, but she reaches out and touches my arm.

"If we can't do anything today, then let's plan for a time for us to get together. Can you have dinner with me?" she asks.

"I don't think so, Kate. I just don't think this is going to work."

"Why not? Why won't you at least talk to me? I had a wonderful time with you. I miss you and I miss Maddox." I melt a little when she mentions Maddox.

"The whole trust issue between us is a pretty big thing. Trust is the foundation in a relationship and when it's broken, then what's the point of continuing the relationship? I can't forgive you just because we had great sex. What happened is not something I'm going to forget just like that." I snap my fingers.

"I didn't want it to ruin the beginning of us." She moves her finger back and forth between us. "I truly am sorry that I never told you that I got the grant. I know I'm a total chicken shit. You and Hunter are the first people who opened yourselves up to me and didn't give up because I didn't talk. It's not easy for me to trust people and then I took your trust and ruined it." She is starting to get emotional.

"You never said anything after you were with us in the car for ten days even when you saw how stressed we were about money. You never said anything when we were sleeping together." I can feel my emotions threatening to spill out and I clench my teeth hoping I can maintain my composure. "You never told us who your father is."

"What the hell does my dad have anything to do with this?" Anger flashes in her eyes.

"Don't pretend you don't know that your father put the squeeze on all the right people to get you that grant. His name is in the paperwork. Did you and your dad just sit around and laugh at how you got money away from people who really need it?" I know I sound like a whiny baby right now, but I'm mad. That man snaps his fingers and suddenly everybody jumps, including the government?

"I have no idea what you're talking about," she says. Her voice is low and surprisingly calm. She folds her arms in front of her. "Before the accident, I hadn't spoken to my father in six years."

"Oh, and when you needed grant money, he just magically appeared and helped you secure it? That doesn't make sense."

"He didn't help me get funding. He wouldn't do that. Do you know why? Because when I came out to my family, they practically disowned me. I was an embarrassment to them. I walked away from them, their money, everything. I've been on my own since I was eighteen. If my dad had anything to do with me getting that grant, I had no idea. I hadn't seen him since my freshman year." Now she's shaking. Her cheeks are getting flush with anger and I realize this really is news to her. It doesn't soften me though.

"Well, it's not as if you shared a lot of yourself with us, Kate. I tried everything to get you to open up to us, to me, but you never did. You never took the time to trust me."

"That's the thing. I did trust you. I opened up to you more than I've opened up to anyone in six years. Now you tell me my father interfered with my paperwork. It makes me remember why I don't like to trust people."

"As far as the grant is concerned, check the backup paperwork. You'll find his name."

She sighs and leans against my desk. "We've actually been working on our relationship again. Not that I'm defending him, but I guess he was just making sure I was making it. This sets us back again." She sounds defeated and now I soften. I know how important family is, especially how delicate it can be when revealing something as personal as your sexual orientation.

"If it means anything, he was very worried when you were in the hospital. If you're working on your relationship, then tread lightly. What's done is done. Family is important. They are there for you for the rest of your life." I can't believe I'm giving her advice, especially since I got screwed during this process. I should have done a better job getting us the funds, simple as that. I really shouldn't blame her, but I'm still hurting and I'm horrible at forgiveness.

"I have to go now. I'm glad you're doing better, Kate. I really am. Thanks for coming down to thank me in person. Good luck with your family and with school." With as much dignity as I can muster, I walk up the stairs, push through the door, and force myself not to turn around. The further I distance myself from her, the more I can feel myself crumble. I need to get to my office before I break down. First day of school and my students don't need to witness me crying.

❖

"So Kate was here?" Hunter asks me. Her eyes are huge with disbelief. She's in my office eating an early lunch. We were able to keep her working for the department by scraping together funds from tiny grants here and there that nobody wanted to apply for because there was more paperwork to fill out than money to be had. Since I was sequestering myself from the world over the summer, I had plenty of time to work on it. It's not as much money as she would have received if we got the MWSE grant, but it pays her bills and she isn't complaining.

"Yeah, and I was a complete ass. Apparently, she didn't know her dad had his hand in getting the grant. She was genuinely shocked at hearing that."

"So she was sad and quiet because she was alone? That's kind of awful," Hunter says. "I mean, good for her for getting out there and being proactive, but that would suck. Can you imagine what it would be like if your family didn't want to have anything to do with you when you told them? I can't." Hunter's right. Kate's had it rough the last six years.

"She wanted to do dinner but I just can't, you know?" I say. Hunter shakes her head at me and rolls her eyes.

"Why do you constantly punish yourself? You know that she's sorry she didn't tell you she got the grant. You know that she didn't know her father was involved. What's there to still be pissed about?"

"It's not that easy. I can't get all involved again. You know trust is hard with me. Once it's broken, it's hard to gain it back.

Besides, she's an hour and a half away so we'd do the long distant thing for how long? Our love life would be weekends and holidays and over the phone. Who would hug me when I have a bad day at work or who would surprise me with dinner? I would miss out on all the little things that make a relationship strong. I need that closeness. You know this about me."

"Welcome to having a relationship, Tris. Tell me which ones have been easy? If they weren't meant to be works in progress, we all would have married the first person we fell in love with," she says. She's right. A relationship is all about give and take and it isn't always going to be easy. "I think you kind of like wallowing a bit. It's easier, huh?" Now, I'm starting to get upset. Hunter is pushing my buttons.

"I just need to chill a bit. I promise I will talk to her, but I need time to process all of this. I was just able to function without her and bam! She shows up looking hot and wants to do dinner. Last time that happened, we were up all night doing everything but talk." I try not to think about how soft her body was to touch and how her skin felt so warm under me, but I can't help it. I close my eyes and allow the quick memory of her perfection to flood my senses again. So passionate, so lovely.

"Hey, lover girl," Hunter says. I open my eyes and stare at her. "Come back to reality okay? I'm starting to get a little uncomfortable here." I smile at her. I've gone from pissed off to sappy in about two minutes. It really was good to see Kate, regardless of our problems. I'm glad she is happy and healthy. After what I saw in the hospital three months ago, and the gorgeous woman in front of me today, I say a silent thank you to God.

"Okay, well I've got class in ten minutes so I'm out of here." I grab my bag and head for the door. "Don't dirty up my office and don't throw away your lunch in my trash. It will stink up the place." I dodge a french fry before I quickly close the door.

CHAPTER TWENTY-ONE

Maddox and I are snuggling on my couch. Friday nights are for ice cream and action packed movies. It's been a grueling week at work and it's time to unwind. I turned down Hunter's invitation for drinks and decided to make it date night with my main man. I need to get away from weather and real life. My phone rings. I look down and my heart jumps when I see it's Kate calling. I freeze, not knowing if I should answer it. My heart says yes, but my brain is trying to smack sense into me. Four rings. Shit.

"Hi." My voice is slow and low. I pause the movie and Maddox looks at me. I think he knows who's on the other end.

"Hi, Tris. How are you?" Kate's very quiet.

"Good. Maddox and I are watching a movie." I'm rambling, trying to fill the void.

"Am I interrupting?" she asks.

"No, I can pause it. What's going on?"

"I wanted to see how you and Maddox are doing. I just went through a folder of photos from our time chasing. I'll have to e-mail you a few of Maddox that you will love. How's Hunter? Is she still with the department?"

"Hunter is still there and we're managing. We did score a few other small grants and awards so she is able to work for the department during off season. That's all she wanted. Plus, there's enough to spread around to others. We're fine, Kate." That's not entirely true, but I'm just tired of the whole thing. Plus, it's nice to hear her voice. I close my eyes remembering her face, her touch, the softness of her long hair. "How is your relationship with your family going?"

"It's slow, but steady. I can't believe how much my little sister has grown up. It's amazing." Her voice is picking up. I smile. At least good things are happening for her.

"I'm happy for you. Family is important." I don't know what else to say.

"How's Maddox?" she asks. She's stretching our conversation and I'm letting her.

"Well, this is the time of year when he, well, we gain weight. He's fat and happy and curled up on the couch next to me," I say. He wags his tail as I pet him.

"Sounds like fun," she says. We're both quiet. We've reached the point of the conversation when it's either going to become personal or one of us will hang up before it gets uncomfortable. Surprisingly, we're both still on the phone. "You know, I miss you." My heart leaps into my throat like it always does when she says sweet things.

"Kate, don't. Let's just keep this simple, okay?"

"Okay. That I can do." She pauses a bit. "How's teaching going?"

"Well, the students don't hate me yet, so I think it's going well."

"How many classes do you have?"

"Only three, but one has a lab. That's where the fun happens." That class is my only salvation. We get to create weather indoors and watch movies and videos of natural disasters. I don't even think that's teaching. That's more like getting paid to have fun with people who enjoy doing what you like to do, too.

"They probably like the videos from the chasing," Kate says.

"Oh, without a doubt. Of course, sometimes my language in the videos is very colorful, but they understand. It's amazing how many of them want to go out with us. It's unfortunate that so many students go out with little to no experience. Hunter gets very upset with the young kids who chase because they don't know what they're doing. They simply want to get a picture of them with a tornado. It's dumb."

"Do you ever let them go out with you and Hunter?"

"No, I don't like to be responsible for anybody else." I cringe and smack my palm to my forehead. That was a stupid thing to say.

"Why did you let me ride with you?" she asks.

I can be noble, or truthful right now. "I thought it was a crappy deal that you were dealt. The circumstances were bad enough, but it wasn't fair that you were going to miss a good season." I shake my head at my own bullshit.

"Hmm. So you wanted to make sure a colleague was going to get the full experience even though she was from a rival school?" I can hear the teasing in her voice.

"Friendly rivals. And, yes, I was extending the olive branch."

"No other reason? None at all?" she asks. I'm quiet for a bit. Now is the time to either be friends or more.

"Well, you're easy on the eyes and Maddox needed a back seat buddy." It's the best I can do, borderline lame, but it's something.

"I'll take that," she says. I can hear her smile.

"So did they say anything to Gage?" I ask.

"He's no longer allowed to use university funds for storm chasing. After what happened to us, he's not ready to get back out there any time soon. He really is sorry. I'm not defending him. I just want you to know that he feels horrible about hurting me and making a bad, rash decision." She takes a deep breath. "I know that you and Hunter wrote letters. The department head showed me your letters. That really made an impact, trust me."

"Well, it wasn't fun for us to watch and just seeing you…" I trail off because I can tell I'm getting emotional. I clear my throat. "It was hard and what he did was idiotic. It's a good thing Hunter had all the communication with him because I was going to kill him."

"Thank you. I tried to stop him, but he was determined to catch the tornado. They said it was a F3. I've never been that scared before. It was nice being with you and Hunter because you always kept us safe. Gage is so wild. I honestly don't think I can do that again," she says.

I don't tell her that I saw her text message to me that she never got to send. She probably doesn't even remember she typed it. "I get that, but you love it. I could see it in your eyes and how excited you were when we saw one, especially the one with the baby goat. Things will change by next season and you'll probably want to get back out next spring." I'm trying to encourage her because I know that she had a fantastic time with us. "Hopefully, it's in your blood."

"We'll see. That was tough. I'm just now able to handle being in a thunderstorm," she says.

"That's pretty normal." Sometimes, I get nervous when the winds pick up around the house. It's one thing to see a tornado in a corn field in the middle of Nebraska, and another to see one headed for your own house. "How did the university handle your injuries? Were you able to finish your classes?" I ask.

She laughs. "Oh, yes. They were afraid I was going to sue so my teachers were very understanding. My classes were extended anyway because of the storm chasing so it really didn't matter. I passed everything. I didn't have much of a summer though."

I settle down into the couch, enjoying the sound of her voice. It's throaty after she laughs and soft when she gets personal. I'm surprised to notice that we've been talking for over an hour.

"It would be nice to see you and Maddox again. I'd like it if you two would come over for dinner or something this weekend."

For the second time tonight, I freeze. "Kate, that's not keeping it simple."

"It's just dinner. A way to thank you for saving me." She sounds sincere and now I'm more worried about my reaction to her than hers to mine. I already know I'm going to say yes.

"We should meet at a restaurant," I say. That's safe.

"But I want to see Maddox, too. We can't do that at a restaurant. I promise to behave when you come over. And I'm a very good cook." I'm already trying to figure out what I'm going to wear. "Would you and Maddox please come by tomorrow and let me cook for you? I'll cook lean so that Maddox doesn't gain any more weight." That makes me laugh.

"But I bring the wine."

"Deal. I'll text you my address and the time. And Tris? Thank you."

CHAPTER TWENTY-TWO

It only takes us an hour and fifteen minutes to reach Kate's apartment. It's in a newer complex with better amenities than most college town apartments. We're early so I put a leash on a reluctant Maddox and take him for a quick walk around the grounds. It's a very pleasant place with two pools, a nice playground, and a basketball court. Maddox does his business and we head back to the Jeep for the wine. Kate's apartment is on the second floor and I have to stop myself from taking the steps two at a time even though Maddox is already at her door. He looks at me, his tail wagging, his tongue hanging out of his happy mouth. Kate opens the door before I even finish climbing the stairs.

"Maddox, come here, boy," she says. He falls in front of her from excitement and offers up his belly for her to rub. She crouches down and loves on him a bit before she turns her attention to me. She stands up slowly, her eyes never leaving mine. "Tristan. Thanks for coming. You look incredible." I watch as her eyes leave mine to travel slowly up and down my body. I shiver at her boldness. Truth be told, I want her to like what she sees. It took me a long time getting ready today. I'm wearing straight leg dark jeans, a three-quarter sleeve black button-down shirt, and black boots. I'm a little warm, but I look hot. Sometimes you have to sacrifice comfort for sex appeal.

Kate's the one who looks fantastic. She's wearing jeans and a tight T-shirt with a tornado on it. I point and smile at it.

"I saw this the other day and had to have it," she says. "Come in, both of you." Maddox jumps around and finds a comfortable place on the couch. I'm just about ready to yell at him to get down, but Kate reaches out and touches my arm. "It's okay. I don't mind at all."

"You should. He already knows you're a softy." I give Maddox a look and his ears go back.

Kate playfully scolds me and reaches for the bottle of wine I'm clutching. "Would you like a glass?" She's very smooth. Sometimes, it's hard to believe she's only twenty-four.

"That would be great. Whatever you're cooking, it smells fantastic," I say.

"Well, since Maddox is looking to shed a few pounds, I thought I'd bake chicken for us. You and I can indulge in the red potatoes and asparagus, but he's only getting the chicken."

"Thanks for thinking of him, too," I say. Hot Mindy from Hunter's Fourth of July pool party pops into my mind. Kate would never have screamed or reacted the way she did with Maddox. She loved him the second she met him.

"I've missed him," she says. She looks at him and he wags his tail at her. He's already hooked. He's not making this easy for me.

"So what have you been working on at school this semester?" I ask. I need to change the subject. She's very comfortable around the kitchen and I remember she's been on her own for six years. Certain things you're forced to learn quickly. I offer my help, but she shoos me away with her chopping knife. She's graceful and fast cutting up vegetables for the salad. She seems so calm, so poised. I'm still quivering inside.

"Well, I didn't lose a lot of time, believe it or not. When you're sitting around feeling sorry for yourself, it's amazing what you can accomplish. I wrote my papers, read a lot, and I even turned in a video of the tornadoes we saw. I kept busy. I only have a few more hours until I get my Master's degree. Woohoo." She celebrates by playfully lifting up the salad tongs in the air.

I smile. "That's a great accomplishment for a twenty-four year old."

"Well, I'm twenty-five now. My birthday was last month," she says.

I didn't know that. "Happy belated birthday, then." I raise my wineglass to hers and we clink them together. I watch her lips touch the glass and swallow hard when I see her tongue flick out to catch a small drop of wine on the rim. My body starts tingling as I remember our few nights together and how her mouth brought me pleasure over and over. This is going to be harder than I thought.

"It was a good birthday. First one I spent with my family in a long time." She smiles and her eyes get a faraway look as she remembers something pleasant. "Yeah, it was nice. Not as nice as yours..." She trails off. I look down at my glass. I'm not ready for this conversation. I can't even make eye contact. I know that if I do, I will be lost in her again.

"I'm glad it was nice. You deserve it." I ignore her comment. I casually walk over to Maddox and sit down next to him. I need distance from her. This is too powerful for me. My eyes are constantly drawn to her, her graceful movements, her calming demeanor. Her hair is down and pulled over one shoulder. It's wavy and lighter than I remember. I want to plunge my hands into it and bring her full lips to my mouth and kiss her again. I miss her warmth and passion and that scares me. This is confusing me. I should still be angry at her, but I'm not.

"Are you sure I can't help?" I ask. She shoots me a lopsided grin.

"It's ready now." She cuts up a giant piece of chicken into smaller bite size pieces and throws the plate in the refrigerator. "For Maddox. It's too warm now." I'm melting. I don't want to fall for her again.

"Maddox is never going to want to leave here."

"He's perfect. I would keep him. Except an apartment really isn't the best place for a dog."

"I did take him for a quick walk around here. It's a cute place. He just doesn't like being on a leash," I say.

"Do you have a large yard?" she asks. We sit down and start eating. Maddox patiently waits beside me for his food.

"I have a house just outside of town with about three acres. It's perfect for him. It's an older farm house that I've been working on for the last couple of years."

"That sounds nice. I'm not very handy. If something breaks around here, I just need to call the manager," she says.

"I'm sure you would be great at any restoration project. It's not that hard. Whenever I get stuck, I call Hunter. She's helped me out of so many sticky situations. Her dad is an electrician. He and I are practically best friends. He's always over. I have yet to finish an electrical problem without needing him. I know he rolls his eyes whenever he sees that I am calling." Kate laughs. "It seems most of my problems are electrical. I can't seem to figure that part out. I can paint anything, nail anything, cut, trim, but I can't stop blowing fuses."

"Maybe it's just really old wiring," she says. She excuses herself to get Maddox's dinner from the refrigerator. He couldn't be happier right now.

"Yeah, we are in the process of switching it all out. I'm happy I know Hunter's dad because if not, this would cost me a fortune."

"I'd like to see it someday," she says.

I look at her and nod. "Maybe next time I'll cook. Or have something very delicious delivered." I'm trying to keep it light. This means that there will be a next date, assuming this is one, too. Surprisingly, the rest of the dinner the conversation flows smoothly. I have agreed to be a resource on her final video project, we like opposing sports teams, she is afraid of spiders and small spaces, and I've shared my secret love of the Harry Potter saga. Before we know it, it's almost midnight.

"It's getting late. Maddox and I should get going. We have a long drive ahead of us." This is the part I don't like. The distance. Even if we start something, then we'll have to face long drives every week. I drive a ton during the chasing season so that doesn't bother me, but not being close does.

"Next time, you can come up and see us," I say. She tucks my hair behind my ear and, just when I think she's going to kiss me, something makes her change her mind and she slowly takes a step back.

"Just say when." She closes the door as Maddox and I walk down the stairs. I climb into the Jeep and Maddox takes the seat next to me.

"That was a good night, huh, boy?" Maddox looks at me and leans over to kiss me. Yeah, we both had a good night. This is the way it's supposed to be. The whole build up, the anticipation, the communication. Now we need to work on trust again and maybe we can get back to where we were.

CHAPTER TWENTY-THREE

"Hey, Dr. Williams wants to see you," Hunter says. Her eyes are wide with a mixture of fear and something else. I stop grading papers and look at her.

"Why do you look worried?" I ask. Now, I'm starting to panic. Hunter never loses her cool. "Do you know something? Do you know what he wants?"

"No. But he seemed tense when he asked me to collect you." She makes quote marks with her fingers after saying collect. That's never good. I rewind my week in my head and I don't remember saying anything inappropriate in class or to a student. All of my paperwork has been turned in on time. I don't know what he could possibly want. I shrug at Hunter and she shrugs back. She walks with me to his office.

"Dr. Williams?" I say, knocking on his door.

"Come in, Tristan," he says. He greets me with a smile, something I'm not expecting at all. Hunter gives me an encouraging thumbs-up and continues walking. I close the door behind me and sit down. Dr. Williams hands me a folder. "This came yesterday. Thought you should take a look at it." I open up the folder and glance through the first few pages. I'm confused.

"Wait. Is this money for our department?" I look through the file again. It sure looks like money for the department. "Is this one hundred thousand dollars?" I'm in disbelief. "What is this? Where did it come from?"

"We don't know. We were hoping you could tell us. It arrived anonymously, but you're the only staff member referenced. Did any of the larger corporations promise you money when you were applying for grants and scholarships?" I think for a moment and shake my head no. I'd remember one hundred thousand dollars.

"I have no idea. I contacted almost everybody within the tri-state area, but nobody promised me anything concrete. This is crazy. I can't believe this." I'm staring at the paperwork, but not really seeing anything. My mind is racing through everybody I reached out to, but I'm coming up empty. This is more money than the MWSE grant.

"Well, whatever you did, thank you." He's smiling at me. He never smiles.

I'm in shock. "Who knows about this?" I ask.

"Nobody yet. Just the dean, me, and you. I thought I would let you break the news to your colleagues."

"We should probably cash it first to make sure it's legit. I mean, who sends an anonymous cashier's check? Can we call this bank? Don't most people want the notoriety?" Dr. Williams chuckles. "Okay, so what now?" I ask. I don't know what to do with this.

"Come up with a budget of sorts. A way to allocate the funds to the different areas you think we need help with. We can meet next week to finalize it." He laughs at that. I'm still very serious. Who does that?

"Okay. I'll work on it." I stand up, and he reaches out and shakes my hand. I'm stunned. I leave his office and head for mine because I know Hunter is there waiting.

"What happened? Are you okay?" she asks when I open the door. I sit down and stare at her. "Oh, my God. Did you get fired? You're white as a ghost."

"No, no. You aren't going to believe this, but we got a hundred grand." She looks as confused as I am. "Yeah, I know. It doesn't make sense. Somebody, we don't know who, donated that money to our department. My name is the only name on the grant or donation or whatever this is."

"Are you shitting me right now?" Hunter jumps up. "What the hell, Tris? We have money? Like money that will keep us here and we can chase next year and all that kind of money?" She's getting more and more excited. She grabs me and suddenly we're both jumping up and down squealing like little girls.

"Yeah, I told Williams he should make sure it clears before we tell everybody. I have no idea who sent it and why they did it anonymously. So let's not celebrate until it clears, okay?"

"Can the two of us at least celebrate tonight? Just in case it's real? I really need this. I've been bummed thinking we weren't going to be able to chase next season."

I smile at her. "Yes, but let's do it at the house. I've got to drop off Maddox. And we don't need to drink and drive. Oh, let's grill. Invite James, too."

"Nah, he's got practice tonight. Okay, I'll swing by the grocery store, pick up some stuff, and be over about five. Is that good?"

"Perfect. See you then," I say. She hugs me one more time and leaves. I still have one more class to teach this afternoon. I'm pretty sure I'm floating right now. I want to blow off class, but I'm the responsible teacher now. I buckle down and head to class. I have to stop myself from skipping. In high heels.

CHAPTER TWENTY-FOUR

The fire pit is warding off the early fall chill as Hunter and I drink beer and eat burgers dripping with cheddar cheese, sautéed mushrooms, and all the condiments I can find in the refrigerator. It is the perfect Friday night. Even Maddox is eating barbecue with us. We aren't trapped in a car with him so he can eat what he wants.

"I still can't believe we got that money. Who did you call? And what or who did you do for that?" Hunter says. I flip her off. We both laugh.

"I love my job, but I'm not doing that to keep it. Well, unless it's somebody from my top five list," I say. Hunter and I have very different lists of famous people we would have sex with if given the opportunity. Hers is littered with musicians, and mine is a compilation of actresses, musicians, and models.

"I just think the whole thing is crazy. That's a lot of money to just give somebody. Hell, even the military has their name plastered all over their grants and theirs isn't nearly that amount. Would your parents or grandparents have done something like this?"

I scoff. "Nobody in my family has that kind of money just lying around. And trust me, I would have to give them at least two or three grandkids before that happens."

"Well, you aren't getting any younger," Hunter says.

"You sound just like my mother."

"Your mother is a smart woman. And speaking of dating, what are your plans for Kate tomorrow?" Hunter asks.

"That so wasn't smooth."

She grins at me and finishes off her beer. "Well?"

"I'm going to cook dinner and just show her around." I'm trying to downplay my emotions, but Hunter knows me better than that.

"Hmmm. And what else? Have you two talked about what's happening?" Hunter knows about last weekend's sort of date.

"We spoke a bit yesterday. I texted her my address and then she called me."

"Have you forgiven her yet?"

"I think I have. I just want to take it slow. There's also the trust thing. Maybe I'm clinging to it, but that hurt. For the first time in a long time, I trusted somebody and she hurt me. Yes, I'm getting over it and I do understand why she did what she did…"

"Then what's the problem? She's beautiful, smart, she speaks our weather language, likes tornadoes, loves Maddox, is great in bed, available, likes you. I just don't understand." Hunter's right. I'm trying to find fault with this fledgling relationship and there really isn't any.

"I'm just nervous I guess. I really like her, but I'm scared that I'll get hurt again. The last four months have sucked." For the first time, I'm honest with Hunter. We always have emotional talks drinking beer around a fire.

"Well, don't let her hurt you. Throw it all out there, tell her you want this to work, but she better make damn sure she doesn't hide something like that again." I lean my head back and look up at the stars.

"Why can't you just have the talk with her first, and then I can have the fun?" I have never done well with heart to heart talks. I get nervous and always say the wrong things.

"Because this is your relationship, not mine." That silences me. Again, she's right.

"Tomorrow should be interesting then." Waiting is the hardest part. All week I've been waiting. I've stopped myself from sending texts because I don't want her to know that I'm thinking about her all of the time. I feel like one of my students. I have my phone on me at all times just in case she calls. During class, department meetings, next to my bed. True to her word, Kate has kept her distance. I'm tired of fighting this thing between us. I need to really forgive and get us back to where we should be. It's nice that Hunter knows her and can give me solid advice. "Do you think we can make this work?"

"The question is do you want to? I think she's everything you've ever wanted. So what that she lives over an hour away? She won't always live far. One day, she'll get her degree and maybe things will be good between you two and she'll move up here."

"Woah, woah. Slow down. Let's get to our second date first before you have us moving in together," I say.

"So get rid of all of the negative energy you're harboring about the whole thing, especially since we have money now, and have a fantastic time tomorrow. I expect a phone call first thing Sunday. Well, not too early because James has a show that I'm going to. High noon. Call me." We clink long necks to seal the deal. I will definitely call her after the date.

"Now that we're done with all of your drama, we need to focus on what's important here. We need to focus on how we're going to spend all of that money," Hunter says. We both laugh. It's still so unbelievable.

"Okay, let's make a list."

"I want a new truck. We destroyed the SUV," Hunter says.

"No. That will take up our whole budget. We really need a minivan," I say.

Hunter spews out her beer. "Oh, my God, no. I'm not driving one of those. We won't be able to drive in and out of ditches. I'll look like a soccer mom. And we'll maybe get to sixty miles per hour. We will never be able to outrun any tornado." She thinks I'm serious.

"Well, we're going to upgrade our equipment and there aren't any SUVs that will house everything I'm looking at. Only a minivan will." The look of shock on Hunter's face is too much and I bust out laughing. "I'm kidding. Thankfully, the better equipment is smaller so we won't have to worry about space. Too bad they don't have a sporty four-by-four minivan."

"You, my friend, would be driving it all by yourself."

"Let's get together early next week before I meet with Williams to figure out what we want and what we can live without. It might be a good idea to set some money aside just in case this is a one time deal. So start thinking of things we need." We are quiet for a moment, each of us spending the money frivolously in our minds.

"If you think I'm going to wear a uniform, think again," Hunter says. I stare at her and wonder how the hell she knows what I'm thinking. I thought Kate's T-shirt with the tornado was cute and was already designing something for us. "No, Tris." I love that she knows me so well.

"Not even a tiny tornado swirling around our school logo?" I ask.

"New subject." She's serious. I might just have to create something for myself. I hold my hands up signaling my surrender.

"Okay, okay. You win. No matching T-shirts. I might get Maddox a collar though." He perks up when he hears his name.

"Yes, we get to go out next year, are you excited?" His tail thumps.

"I need to get going. James is anxious to celebrate tonight," Hunter says. "Come on, I'll help you clean."

"Don't worry about it. I have a lot of nervous energy to expel. Cleaning is next on my list. I'll be doing it all day tomorrow." I hope Kate likes the house. I've poured a lot of my heart and soul into it. "I'll call you Sunday at high noon." Hunter hugs me and heads home. Maddox and I hang around the fire a little bit longer and enjoy the chilly night air and the bright stars. What a crazy week this has been.

CHAPTER TWENTY-FIVE

I'm pacing and looking out the window every minute. Maddox is starting to follow me. He thinks it's a game. I've been watching the clock all day. Kate is due in ten minutes and I've worked myself into a bundle of nervous energy waiting for her. The second I sit down, I see headlights pull into the drive. I wait until I hear a car door close before I open the door. Maddox bolts outside via the doggy door and is dancing around Kate.

"Four paws down, Maddox," I say, pointing at the floor. He immediately settles down and stops jumping. Kate is holding a light jacket and a bottle of wine high up in the air to avoid Maddox's onslaught of attention. "I'm sorry. He's very excited to see you." She smiles and heads toward the stairs. I'm mesmerized by her. She's wearing a fitted wool dress and knee high leather boots. Her hair is pulled up and back, tendrils hanging down. I look like I'm headed to the grocery store in my jeans and black sweater.

"Can I come in?" She asks. I've been so busy staring at her, I've completely forgotten my manners.

"Oh, my God, yes. Come on in." I retreat back inside with Kate right behind me. She's tall in those boots and I'm trying hard not to think about her legs or how badly I want to touch them again.

"This is an incredible house, Tristan," she says. I watch her as she looks around, appreciating all of my hard work. I can't help but smile.

"Now you know what I do when I'm not working or chasing." We smile at one another. I reach out to take the wine and her jacket. "I'll give you a quick tour of the place. We have a few minutes before dinner is ready." I cheated and ordered food from a very nice restaurant in town, but I did make the bread and it still has a few minutes to bake.

She loves the ornate woodwork and I watch as she touches everything. "Did you carve all of this?" she asks. There is surprise in her voice and as much as I want to take the credit, I don't.

"No. A lot of the woodwork is from a torn down theatre from the university. I just repurposed it. I cleaned, sanded and stained the handrails, chair rails, and moldings. Some of it is rather fancy, but I think it works." She laughs and nods.

"Definitely. I think it's great." She follows me around, truly appreciating my house. I'm bursting with pride. I'm a little hesitant to go upstairs because the bedrooms are all up there, but she continues the tour without me and I'm forced to follow. The view is definitely nice as we climb the stairs. I'm itching to touch her curves again, but I keep my hand on the railings. At the top of the stairs, I tell her to turn left and we peek into the three bedrooms and one bathroom on that side. "What's behind this door?" I stop her before she opens it. She smiles at me. "What is it, Tris?"

"I'm saving this for last. You'll see." I steer her to the right and show her my office and the master suite.

"Your bedroom is beautiful," she says. I watch her run her hands over the bedposts and across my bedspread as she heads toward the windows. "I can understand why you spend all of your spare time at home. It's fantastic."

"I appreciate it more and more the longer I'm on the road, trust me." I love that Kate gets to see this side of me. Not too many people do. My phone beeps and I look down. It's the timer. "I have to get the bread out. Let me run downstairs real quick and get it out of the oven." I slip past her and head down the stairs. I'm a little nervous about leaving her in my bedroom. That's my personal space and Kate and I are just starting to get used to one another again. Not that I think she is going through my panty drawer or that I will find her naked on my bed, but again, she's learning a lot about me and I have yet to break through all of her walls.

The food is ready, but I want to show Kate what's behind the secret door before we come back downstairs. I take the steps two at a time, anxious to get back to her. I watch as she holds up my silver necklace, gently holding it as she tries to read the inscription on the flower pendant.

"My grandmother gave me that when I was a little girl. It means blossom in Cherokee," I say. She hands it to me.

"It's beautiful. You should wear it."

I laugh. "She gave it to me on my tenth birthday. It hasn't matched anything in my wardrobe in fifteen years."

"Well, I like it." She watches as I put it into the jewelry box. "You have quite a bit of jewelry." She sounds surprised.

"I told you I'm not a Neanderthal the rest of the year. You actually got to know me at my worst. Or best, depending on how you look at it." She's very close to me. Her eyes drop to my mouth. I find myself leaning toward her and pull gently back. Now is not the time. "Are you ready to see the best part of the house?" She nods and I take her hand to guide her back out to the mysterious door. I don't know why I reached out for her hand, but I'm glad that I did because I like her warmth against me. I've missed her. She's even closer to me because we're holding hands. I don't want to let go. We reach the door and I turn around to face her. She is so close to me. I can see her pupils dilate. I don't think I'm going to be able to keep my hands off of her tonight. I can feel my resolve slipping and the need for her to be naked in my arms growing. I know that if we start kissing, we will end up a pile of hot sex right here on the floor and I don't want that. Or so I keep telling myself.

"I'm not done with this yet, but I'm sure you will understand where I'm going with it." I reluctantly drop her hand and open the door. There are a dozen steps leading up and I motion for Kate to enter. I flip on the light switch and follow her up.

"This is amazing." She stands in the middle of the loft and slowly turns. I've created a solitude room with comfy chaise lounges and old bookcases full of all types of books. The ceiling is slanted and the room isn't symmetrical, but it's a great private room with windows that let in a ton of light during the day. "This is the attic?"

"No. The attic is next door." I point to the wall to our north. "This was part of it at one time, but the previous owner did most of the work. I just finalized it all. I found these incredible bookshelves and decided this would be my sanctuary. I'm not a reader, but I'm a napper and this is a great place to be when it's raining."

"It's fantastic. I would be up here every day. You know how much I like to read. And I would write in my journal up here."

"Is that what your notebook is? A journal? I didn't know if you were writing or drawing or just taking notes in it."

She looks shyly at me. "It's a great way for me to get my feelings out when I can't say them. I'm trying to do better. Now that I'm with my family more, I'm better at communicating. I don't need my journal as much." I'm happy for her, but sad that she needed a journal in order to communicate.

"Well, I can see a difference." I realize I really do notice a big change in her. She's friendlier, talks more, and seems happier. "Let's get down to the kitchen. I'm getting hungry. I know, I know, no surprise there." She laughs and we head back downstairs. She helps me bring the food to the table and raises her eyebrow at me when she notices the take out boxes.

"I'm not a good cook. I can grill but since the weather is iffy tonight, I decided dry inside is better than cold and wet out there. You'll like it. It's healthy, except for the bread. I did bake that from scratch though." I can bake. I actually love to bake.

"It smells great. I'll even have some bread since you made it yourself," she says. I pour the wine as she settles into the chair. "I'll skip the butter though." I look at her like she's crazy. Who skips butter on fresh, hot homemade bread? I shake my head at her. She laughs.

"So do you cook every night at home?" I ask.

"No. It's hard to just cook for myself. I might bake chicken and have it twenty different ways throughout the week. That's usually how I spend my Sundays."

"You should be watching football on Sundays. And Saturdays, too. I'm a complete loaf during the winter. At least this winter I'll work on the basement. I need to hang more sheetrock before I do the finishing touches."

"Do you have a separate storm shelter or just the basement?" Kate asks.

"I have a five by eight storm shelter under the front porch. It's made of concrete and is perfect for bad weather. The rest of the basement is kind of a playground. I have a pool table, dart board, big television, and a small bar. By spring, it will be done and ready for guests. Right now, it's pretty rough."

"I'm glad you have a storm shelter. It has to be scary being far away from neighbors," she says.

"It's not too bad. My neighbors are friendly and we always help out when there's a problem. Plus, I have Maddox and a few shotguns around here. I'm not worried about people. I'm more worried about wild animals," I say.

"I was thinking that when I saw Maddox's doggy door. Do you ever have unwanted guests?"

I laugh. "One time, when Maddox was still a puppy, a raccoon crawled in and Maddox thought it was for him to play with. He couldn't understand why I was screaming and why the raccoon was hissing. It took forever to get the raccoon out of here."

"I can't wait until I get my own place and I can have pets. I did have a kitty growing up, but she ran away. You have the perfect set up here. The house is back away from the road and you have land where Maddox can run around and be a dog," she says.

"You can always get another kitty. They are pretty easy and don't mind the indoors," I say. Our conversation changes smoothly from topic to topic and I find Kate absolutely charming. She's very quick witted and I admire her intelligence. I grab another bottle of wine from the rack.

"I should stop. I need to drive home tonight," Kate says.

"Well, it's raining harder so I don't think you are going anywhere tonight," I say. The look she gives me makes me almost drop the bottle. "I mean, I have so many extra bedrooms and you're more than welcome to one." I don't tell her that I ran out and bought an extra toothbrush, razor, and new towels just in case she did decide to stay. I grab my phone and show her Doppler. "See? It's not letting up anytime soon. I'd rather you stay put." I'm leaning over her as we look at the screen. She smells like flowers and vanilla and it's so hard not to touch her.

"Okay, if you don't mind," she says.

"Not at all. So, hand me your glass and let's go sit in the living room." I allow her to sit where she wants and I put my glass on the table beside hers. I head over to the fireplace and start a fire. I know she is watching me and I'm nervous, but I want her to look at me. I want her to talk about us, bring up our past and talk about a future. She's being so patient with me and sometimes I think maybe we're just going to be friends, but then she gives me a look that shakes me to my core. I'm so confused.

"I love fires. Thank you. This is a nice night," she says. I smile as she hands me my wine. I leave a gap between us and Maddox takes the opportunity to jump on the couch between us.

"Get down, boy." He's already fallen out on the couch with his paws in the air. Kate's rubbing his chest and whispering to him. I'm jealous of him right now. I have a nice fire going, had a great meal, and that should be my head in Kate's lap, not his. I sigh. Lucky dog.

"I can get him down if you want," Kate says. She looks sad so I let him stay on the couch. I'll just sulk for a bit. I have all night to figure out if I'm going to make a move or not.

"We can watch a movie if you want," I say.

"Or we can just sit here and talk," she says.

I smile at her. "That's a better idea." We slip into a conversation about movies. I'm surprised to find out that she hasn't seen a movie in the theatre in years.

"I'm glad you're working on your relationship with your family. It seems like you've had it rough without them. I told Hunter I thought you had an old soul, but now I think you were just lost for a bit." She smiles at me and I panic when I see tears in her eyes. "Oh, Kate. I'm sorry. I didn't mean to upset you, really. It's just that I'm figuring things out about you and it's nice getting to know you. Please don't cry." She laughs, her way of alleviating the tension she's feeling.

"I'm sorry I'm emotional right now. I'm overwhelmed with good feelings. My family, you, Maddox. It's nice and it's just been so long since I've reciprocated any feelings. I sometimes just don't know what to do but cry." I want to hug her right now, but I can't because the beast is between us. Instead, I hold my glass up to give her a toast. "To you and new beginnings."

"Here's to second chances," she says and clinks my glass. We fall into a comfortable silence. "So, does Maddox go outside when it's raining like this?"

"He has no choice. I know he's prolonging it because he knows he has to stay in the mud room until he's dry. He's got it too good right now. I wouldn't want to leave either." Kate looks at me in surprise and I freeze. I can't believe I just said that. I begin back peddling. "I mean, he's pretty comfortable and happy." I decide to shut up. I can't get out of this one so I just ride it out. "So, what are your plans for the rest of the weekend?" Thankfully, she allows the change of topic.

"Well, it won't be watching football." I laugh at that. "I have some school work to do and then I'm not sure what else. What about you?"

"I'm going to work on the basement while football is on. We're kind of rained in this weekend and I need to get away from everybody. This has been a rough, but exciting week." I suddenly remember about the anonymous donation, but I'm a little hesitant to bring up school funds. This is such a nice night so I skip over it.

"I can still go if you want to be alone," she says. I watch her lean over Maddox's head and put her glass on the table. She pulls a clip out of her hair. I watch as the pile of beautiful hair falls softly down her back. "I was starting to get a headache with it pulled up."

"You have such beautiful, soft hair." Crap. I think the wine has dissolved my filter. I, too, put my glass down. "I've always wanted long hair, but I get so impatient. This is the longest I've had it and it's not that long." At least my ponytail is longer than it was during the summer. My hair is just past my shoulders now. Kate's is halfway down her back.

"You have thick hair and it looks nice straight. I have to curl my hair if I leave it down. That's why during the summer you always saw me with it pulled back somehow." She looks completely relaxed right now. Her arm is on the back of the couch, her body angled toward me with her beautiful legs crossed. I can't help but look at her. She's beautiful. I need Maddox to get off of the couch. I play it off by looking at my watch.

"It's getting late. Come on, Maddox. Time to go outside one last time." He's not happy with me. He ignores me until I snap my fingers. He slowly slides off the couch and I march him to the mud room and point to his doggy door. "The sooner you go, the sooner you can be back." He slowly slips through the door and I hit the kitchen to clean up.

"Do you want my help?" Kate stands in front of me and I almost reach out to her, momentarily forgetting we aren't there yet.

"Thanks, but no. It will only take a few minutes. I have to dry Maddox off so I didn't want to sit back down. Go enjoy the fire. I'll be there in a minute." I watch her walk back over to the couch, enjoying the slight sway of her hips and the tightness of her dress. This is going to be a tough night for me.

❖

"What is it about midnight and us?" I say. The clock above the mantel softly chimes twelve times. "Come on. Let's go upstairs before we both fall asleep very uncomfortably on this couch. Find a bedroom upstairs you want while I lock up and turn off lights. Maddox, go with Kate." He happily obliges and trots off with her. This is the awkward part of the night. Good nights are tough. I find Kate in the bedroom closest to the master bedroom. "Let me find you something to wear." I head to my closet and dig around for pajamas.

"It doesn't have to be anything fancy. I'll take a T-shirt." I jump and turn around, surprised that she's in my closet.

"You scared me." My heart is pounding because I was startled, but now it's because she's so close to me. She is barefoot, but still wearing her dress.

"I didn't mean to. I wanted to let you know that I'll be fine in just a T-shirt." She's close enough that I can see the flecks of brown in her blue eyes. I slowly back away and grab the first T-shirt I find. I also give her a pair of boxers and warm socks.

"Just in case you get cold." I put the stack of clothes between us. She has no choice but to take it. "I also put out a toothbrush and fresh towels in the bathroom. Just let me know if you need anything else."

"Can Maddox sleep with me?" Really? Maddox?

"Sure, but know he's a bed hog," I say.

She smiles and her eyes drop down to my mouth. I automatically lick my lips. "Thanks for a very nice evening," she says. She doesn't move. I'm trapped in my closet. This is about to get uncomfortable unless I push past her or cave into my desire and kiss her. Just when I'm ready to make my move, she walks out of the closet. I shake my head at my own indecisiveness. She was right in front of me, in my personal space, and I just stood there like an idiot. I sigh and walk out of the closet. She's not in my room anymore. I fall on my bed. This is so hard.

❖

I can hear the storm outside, but that's not what wakes me up. Maddox has his nose very close to my face and I can feel his breath. I roll away from him. What is he doing off the bed? He was with Kate so why is he here?

"Maddox, what are you doing here?" I can hear his tail thumping.

"Are you awake?" Kate asks me from the other side of the bed. Lightning lights up the room and I see her jump.

"Kate, are you okay? What's wrong?"

"I just…I'm scared of the storm. Ever since the accident, I have a hard time sleeping through bad weather. Can I stay here with you? I can sleep on the chaise or at the end of the bed." Now she's being ridiculous.

"No, no. Come on in," I say. I open up the covers on the other side of the bed and she quickly slips in.

"Thanks."

I'm completely awake now. Even though we aren't touching, I can feel her body heat. A loud clap of thunder rumbles overhead and I feel the bed tremble. Kate is so scared, she is shaking. I automatically roll to her and scoop her into my arms.

"Shh, Kate. It's okay. You're safe here." I stroke her hair until I feel her relax against me. She jumps a little bit when we hear thunder, but it's not as bad. It never dawned on me that she would have trouble with storms after being in a tornado. Completely understandable. I snuggle up closer to her. She's warm and soft against me and I have to constantly remind myself she is here for comfort not to be seduced. Eventually, I hear her breathing even out and I know she is asleep. I'm wide awake as every part of her touching me reminds me of a different time when I could touch her anywhere. How many times did I wake her up just so we could have sex before morning? I smile at the memories. At least we are working on a relationship now. I do miss her and we'll have the weekends to see one another. The storm has died down and now it's just a gentle rain falling down. My perfect sound. I feel myself drifting away and I smile as I give in to sleep with a beautiful woman in my arms.

CHAPTER TWENTY-SIX

I wake to Kate wrapped all around me. Her head is on my shoulder, her arm across my chest, and her legs entwined with mine. I have no idea what time it is, I just know that I'm not moving until she wakes up. This is nice. For a second, I pretend this is our life. Together, close, happy. Even Maddox is pleased. He stares at me, his tail wagging.

"Go outside," I say. My voice is low so that I don't wake Kate. I swear he nods at me and makes his way downstairs. Kate stirs in my arms.

"I'm sorry." She weakly tries to untangle herself from me, but gives up. She's asleep again. I smile. At least she's comfortable. We lay like that for quite a long time until I have to slip out from under her to go to the bathroom. I decide to make her breakfast. I watch her sleep for a moment before I head downstairs. So peaceful, so sweet. I can feel my heart swell watching her and I quickly leave, my feelings too close to the surface. I need distance.

Thank God she doesn't like a lot of fatty foods. Breakfast should be easy. I cube up some fruit and make pancakes. It only takes me twenty minutes. I throw a pancake at Maddox as I make my way upstairs with the tray. She is still asleep, this time she's on her stomach, my pillow clutched close to her side.

"Kate, Kate," I whisper. She opens her eyes a bit and smiles at me. She falls back to sleep. Oh yes, I do remember how she hates waking up. "I made you breakfast. Wake up." Nothing. She doesn't stir. I shrug and decide to take a quick shower. The plate warmers will keep the pancakes warm until I'm done. I function better after I'm clean. As much as I want to stay in the shower, I keep it quick and am back to the bed in ten minutes. This time she is sitting up, the tray across her legs and she's munching on a strawberry. "That's probably the fastest I've ever seen you wake up." I crawl into bed next to her and grab my plate. She smiles at me. For a second I think she's going to kiss me, but she leans back and focuses her attention back to her plate.

"I'm not a morning person at all. This is so nice. Thanks for breakfast in bed." She runs her hands over her hair, smoothing down the imperfections. She's adorable.

"You still look great," I say. She smiles shyly at me. She passes me the syrup and we eat breakfast in silence. I know she is still trying to wake up and I'm still trying to calm my heart. At least we are comfortable around each other. "I think it's going to rain all day. The rain gauge says we got about two and a half inches."

"I'm sorry I busted in here last night. I get scared whenever I hear wind. I think it's another tornado. I know I'm being crazy."

I hold up a hand to stop her. "I completely understand. I would be afraid of winds, too, if I was hit by a tornado. I'm glad you came to me."

"Thanks. Since my apartment is sandwiched between two stories, I don't hear the wind as much."

We finish our breakfast and I take the tray off of Kate's lap. I'm not quite sure what happens next so I take everything downstairs to give us both a moment. When I return, she's in the guest shower. I know she isn't going to want to wear her dress again, so I dig around for yoga pants, a sweatshirt, and some shoes. She's too slight for my jeans. At least we are close in shoe size. I knock on the door and enter.

"I'm leaving clothes that you can wear if you don't want to wear your dress again. Nothing fancy, but they're clean and comfortable."

"Thanks again."

I reluctantly leave. Fighting this attraction is getting harder and harder by the minute. I head downstairs to clean up the kitchen and give her space. She comes downstairs about twenty minutes later, dressed in the clothes I left for her. She looks relaxed and soft.

"I promise I won't tell a soul that you're wearing an OU sweatshirt," I say. She laughs.

"I was tempted to hit your closet again for another sweatshirt, but decided this one isn't so bad after all." She sits down at the breakfast bar and I hand her another cup of coffee, two creams, two sugars. "I'll leave here in a bit so that you can get your work done."

"It's no big deal. Stay as long as you like. It's nice having you around." I smile because I mean it. "Unless you have to get back to work on your own projects. I know you have a lot going on right now."

"I actually have my paperwork in my bag in the car. I can work on it for a bit here. I might even need your help."

"Sounds great. I'll work downstairs and you can set up anywhere. My office or even right here." There is a ton of room on the breakfast island.

"I'll just work right here. Maddox can keep me company. It's not raining as hard right now so I'm going to grab my bag." She heads out the door and I remember I need to call Hunter. It's not noon, so I send her a quick text telling her about the night. I don't want her to worry about me, or worse, assume the best case scenario. Kate's back in a flash and I help move things around for her to get settled.

"Well, I'll be downstairs if you need me. Maddox, stay."
I head downstairs with sanding down sheetrock mud on the agenda. I'm very aware of Kate and it's a comforting feeling. I know that I trust her again and now it's just a matter of finding out what she's looking for. What does she want besides really good sex? Is she ready for a relationship? Is she going to want to commute back and forth for who knows how long? Does she even feel that way about me? I feel like she's wanted to kiss me several times during our prolonged second date so I'm pretty sure the interest is there, but is the commitment?

I'm surprised to see that I've sanded the entire wall already. Two and a half hours flew by. Maddox suddenly by my side surprises me.

"What are you doing down here, boy?"

"We thought you could use a break," Kate says. They're both down here. "This is going to be beautiful when you get done with it, Tris."

I beam with pride. "Thanks. I've put a lot of time into this house and I plan to enjoy it for a long time."

"Are you getting hungry or anything?" she asks. She's standing close to me, looking at the wall, but the only thing I can focus on is her nearness. I'm suddenly conscious that I'm covered in grit and sweat. I got rid of my sweatshirt about ten minutes into this project and I'm wearing a thin T-shirt that I can't wait to shed.

"Sure, I can stop for a bit. I need a quick shower. Do you mind?" I ask.

"Go ahead. I can wait." I bolt up the stairs without waiting for her. I head to the bathroom and gasp when I see my reflection. I'm covered in white dust. No wonder she was fine with me taking a quick shower. I can't get under the hot water soon enough. It takes me longer to clean up than I expected. I turn the water off and grab my towels. I wrap one around me and dry my hair with the other. I need to figure out what to wear.

"I can't do this," Kate says. I stifle a scream and clutch my towel tighter around me. Kate is sitting on the edge of the claw foot tub when I exit the shower. I want to get mad at her for her scaring me, but the look on her face is so vulnerable. My spirits are instantly crushed.

"Do what?" I ask. I think I know what she means, but I need to know for sure. My heart is beating frantically in my chest as if trying to flee. She walks over to me, cups my face in her hand.

"I can't be around you and not want you," she says. "I need you to forgive me. I want this, all of this, with you. Will you ever trust me again?" She places a soft, sweet, gentle kiss on my lips. Before I have the chance to enjoy it, her mouth has moved over to my cheek, down to my neck, before she finds my mouth again. "Please. Please forgive me." Her voice breaks and is full of emotion. Tears spring to my eyes when I hear her pleading. Her lips are barely touching mine as she waits for my answer. I don't hesitate and pull her close to me, my lips hard against her. She whimpers against me and I feel her hands clutching my towel. I find that I can't get close enough to her. My towel and her clothes are in the way. I pull away from her long enough to steady both of us.

"I forgave you a long time ago." I take her by the hand and lead her to the bed. I sit down and pull her to stand between my legs. I lean into her and hold her while I relish the feel of her strong fingers in my hair.

"Why didn't you say anything to me?" she asks.

"I wanted to be sure this is what you want, too," I look up at her. She slides down until she's on her knees in front of me and we are almost eye to eye.

"I've wanted this since the first day I met you." She leans up and kisses me. I hate that we are so far apart and only our lips are touching. "I'm so sorry I screwed up." I silence her by kissing her again. I gently pull her up and onto me so that we are both on the bed.

"Didn't we toast to second chances and new beginnings last night?" I ask. She smiles at me. Her gorgeous hair falls around me as she leans in for another kiss. I need to feel her skin against mine so I lift her sweatshirt up a bit. My towel is almost undone and the second I feel her stomach against mine, I tear the towel off completely. She moans at the contact, too. "Take your clothes off." She straddles me and sheds the sweatshirt and T-shirt until she is in her lacy bra and my yoga pants. I run my hands up over her flat stomach until I reach lace. "This, too." I think it's fair that if I'm naked, she should be, too. She doesn't hesitate. I've missed her body. Her perfectly smooth, pale skin quivers under my touch. "Are you cold? Let's get under the covers." I move to the side, but she shakes her head.

"I'm not cold, it's just nice that you're touching me again." Her words are melting me. I pull her down until she is flush against me. Then I flip us over so that I am on top. She gasps. I smile and kiss her slowly, deeply until I hear her moan. Her hips are moving against me. I need that heat against me, too. I reach down and tug on her pants until she helps me take them off. She is gloriously naked next to me and I want to touch her everywhere at once. I want to make sure she is real, that this is happening. Her skin is flushed with passion and her body presses into my hand with every caress. I run my hands down her sides as I nestle myself between her legs.

"I've missed you." It's simple and honest and makes her cry. This time I let her. I know that she has to get rid of the bad to accept the good. I kiss some of the tears that slide down her face. "Only good things now, okay?" Her blue eyes are somber as she looks up at me, but she smiles.

Once I feel her body settle down, I start kissing her again. This time I don't stop. My mouth devours her, my hands roam her body, touching her curves, memorizing each valley. I'm in complete control and I'm not giving it up until I feel her explode in my arms. Her hips dig into mine, grinding for friction. My mouth leaves hers and I start a path down her body, my tongue moving across her breasts, licking her nipples until she moans and pushes my mouth closer to her, begging me to suck them.

I can't get enough of her. Her taste, her smell, her passion. I roll to the side and glide my hands down her body until they reach her warm, wet pussy. She spreads her legs further apart for me and I don't hesitate. I slide one finger inside of her, moaning at how tight and wet she is. I slip in another finger and her back arches. She's too tight for a third so I move in and out of her while sucking the side of her neck. Her legs are moving up and down, her heels trying to dig into my bed. I move my weight to between her legs, my hand still between us. She wraps her legs around me, locking her ankles. I balance myself up on my free arm and watch her face as my fingers continue moving in and out of her. She is beautiful. So giving, so free. She licks her lips. As hard as she tries to keep her eyes open, she can't. With every thrust she arches her back, moans and clutches me closer. I could stay like this forever.

I lean down and kiss her when I hear her breathing increase. Her body starts shaking and I know she is close. I don't slow down or speed up, I go deeper. I feel like I'm bruising both of us, but she moans delightfully and I know it's a pleasurable pain. She comes loudly, her sweaty body quivering against mine. It's a beautiful sight. Eventually, she relaxes and releases her legs and arms from my body. I place tiny kisses on her face, her neck. After a few quiet moments next to her, I feel her smile against my cheek and look up at her.

"What?" I don't really need an answer.

"You're incredible." She leans up and kisses me then falls back down. Her hand rests on my shoulder, caressing my arm as we lie there enjoying the aftermath of really incredible makeup sex. "You got stronger." I'm confused by that statement, but as I feel her fingers touch the lines of the muscles in my arm, I realize she means physical strength.

"Well, I threw a lot of time into working on the basement. Lifting sheetrock, mudding it, sanding it. It's been a good workout I guess." I shrug like it's no big deal, but I'm happy she likes my new definition.

"Yeah, I like it a lot. Very sexy. You're stronger, more in control." I decide at that moment to work out every day. In the past, it was always back and forth between us. She would get aggressive, then I would. This time, I didn't let her. I needed that.

"Did I hurt you?" I know I was roughish right before she came.

"No. It was perfect. I promise." I lean down and kiss her softly. The last twenty-four hours have been incredible. "What's that noise?" she asks. We both still and listen. It's music. Hunter is calling me. I know it's her from the song.

"That's just Hunter dying to know how my night went," I say.

"Do you need to get it?" she asks.

"No. I can call her later." I lean down and kiss her again.

"How did your night go?" She leans up and nips my neck and chin.

"The night part was stressful, but today was…" I pause and kiss her. "Today was the best day of my life." It sounds corny, but it's true. I've never felt so at peace before and yet so alive with energy.

"And it's not even over yet." She grabs my hair and gently brings me down to her lips for a searing kiss. "I have to make sure I leave by eight if I want to get home at a decent hour." She tells me after we break apart. It's two in the afternoon now. We have plenty of time to enjoy one another before she has to leave.

"Let's make some lunch, then figure out the rest of the day," I say. She responds by running her hand down my body, over my hips, and slipping her fingers between my legs. I fall backward only moments before she pounces on me. Lunch can wait. I can't.

❖

"Why haven't you answered my texts? Do you know that I drove by, saw a car, assumed it was Kate's and left?" Hunter says. She's upset and I'm an ass for not calling her sooner.

"I'm sorry. Kate and I had a lot to get through and talk about and it just took a while." Okay, so most of the stuff we had to get through was what she likes in bed and what I like, but Hunter doesn't have to know.

"Where's Kate now?" she asks.

"She's in the kitchen. We're going to eat a quick dinner, then she's going to leave. She only stayed because it was getting late and it rained a ton. I didn't want her to drive in it. It's a good thing she did because we talked about our relationship today."

"What's the status?"

"Everything is good. We're both going to work on it."

"Hot damn. That's great," she says. I know it's right because Hunter knows Kate. She would never approve of someone if she didn't truly feel like she was a good fit for me. Of course, this is the first woman Hunter has liked enough to push us together.

"We will talk about it tomorrow at work, okay? Let me have these last few hours with Kate. I promise I will tell you everything." Hunter grunts something and then hangs up. I don't blame her for being mad at me. I would have done the same thing if I was in her shoes.

I look at Doppler and walk into the kitchen. "What time is your first class tomorrow?"

"At nine. Why?" Kate asks.

"Well, it's going to start raining again within the next hour and end about eleven tonight. You could stay and just leave early in the morning. I have to be at school by seven thirty so I have to get up early." I look up at her. I think for a minute I'm being too pushy, but she agrees.

"No, that's a great idea. If you don't mind."

I smile at her. "I can help you with your homework if you want."

"I do need to work on that for a bit. I'd love your help. It's about global warming and the effect it has, if at all, on natural disasters." I roll my eyes at her and fake yawn. She laughs.

"Yeah, I know it sounds awful and overdone, but I have a different twist on it." Kate's very smart and I'm excited because I know she will challenge me. I'm sure her research will blow me away. There's nothing sexier than a smart woman.

CHAPTER TWENTY-SEVEN

Drink this on the road. It's loaded with yummy caffeine and will keep you awake. Text me when you get home safely. I'll be in class, but I'll have my phone out on my desk, okay?" I've walked Kate to her car and I'm trying to let her go, but I'm having a hard time. I pull her close to me for another kiss.

"I'm never going to get to class on time if you keep kissing me." She leans into me for another kiss.

"Apparently, I'm not the only one who's enjoying this," I say. I kiss her one last time and take a step back. She finally slips inside her SUV. It's very nice, the newest model. "I didn't pay attention to your car before. This is gorgeous." It's the perfect model for chasing.

"Since my accident, my dad has been pretty insistent on my safety. He junked my Honda when I was in the hospital and got this for me instead. It's one of the safest," she says.

"It's one of the nicest," I say. "I need to think about this for an upgrade. Oh, did I tell you that we received an anonymous donation a few days ago? Dr. Williams is asking me to budget it." I keep my tone light so she won't fixate on it.

"That's great. All of your hard work paid off." She frowns and I stop her.

"Don't think about it. Go. Get on the road. I'll talk to you tonight," I say. I tap the top of the car and she slowly pulls away. I stand in the driveway and watch until her car disappears over the hill. Best weekend ever.

❖

"I forgive you, but I want all the details right now," Hunter says. She shuts the door and plops down in my guest chair. I look up from grading quizzes and smile at her. "Ah-ha! That good, huh?"

"It was fantastic. She stayed the whole weekend and it was really nice. We talked, we cried, we had incredible sex, we slept, we ate, we had incredible sex. It was perfect."

"That's great. I'm so happy for you."

"Me, too. I think it's going to work. So, have you thought about the funds?" I try to change the subject, but Hunter's smart.

"No, you aren't getting off that easy. Details," she says. I sigh and give her a play by play account of the entire weekend, minus the sex. I brush over that because she doesn't need to know everything.

"So when she crawled into bed with you half naked you didn't do anything?"

"She was genuinely scared. She was shaking. You were there when she got hurt. You saw what happened. I'd be scared if that happened to me, too."

She nods in understanding. "Do you think she'll chase again?"

"She graduates in December so if she does, it won't be with OSU," I say.

"Maybe she'll want to come out with us," Hunter says. Interesting point.

"Maybe. Okay, now can we talk about the money?" I know that the funds are legit because Dr. Williams left a message for me first thing this morning. We have a meeting scheduled for Wednesday.

Hunter and I decide to split the money into funds for the next two seasons. The equipment upgrades won't be too much. The insurance already covered the SUV so we have that money to buy another vehicle. We decide to stick with the same model. After seeing OSU's vehicle get slaughtered, it doesn't make sense to plug a lot of money into a car that is no match for Mother Nature. After about an hour and several lists later, we have our final decision and I'm excited to share it with Dr. Williams.

"And this will at least keep you here for the next couple of years," I say.

"Thank God because I don't want to work for the news," Hunter says.

"Hey, why don't you work on your graduate degree? You know you have a job for at least the next two years here. After you're done, you can teach here during off season, or somewhere close by." I'm excited. Hunter would be a great teacher. She chews on the inside of her cheek so I know she is mulling over the idea.

"That's not a bad idea. As a matter of fact, that's a great idea. And if OU doesn't have a place for me, then somebody else will," she says. I'm not keen on the idea of losing Hunter, but I wouldn't want to hold her back either.

"Go talk to Nadine and she'll help you plan classes and stuff," I say. Nadine is the staff counselor. She helped me with my schedule several years ago. "She's great and she'll tell you if it's doable or not." Hunter stands and scoops me up in a bear hug.

"You're awesome. Thanks. Now, get back to work." I laugh at her enthusiasm and focus my attention back on grading quizzes when she leaves. My phone beeps.

Thanks again for an incredible weekend.

I smile and notice the time.

Hey, aren't you supposed to be in class? Why are you texting?

It's all stuff I already know.

Trust me your teacher knows what you're doing. We know everything.

Maybe that will scare her into paying attention. My phone doesn't beep for a while and I think we are done.

I liked waking up with you.

That melts my heart.

I liked you touching me. I liked touching you.

I sit up straight and look around. I don't know why because I'm alone in my office with the door shut. Nobody can see me or read my texts.

I liked it too. I already miss you.

I try to keep it somewhat light. We're too fresh for me to bare my soul to her. All in good time.

When will I see you again?

This weekend for sure. I can come down or you can come up.

Your house is bigger. More space for Maddox. Can I come up there?

And I melt some more. She's worried about Maddox's comfort. I don't know of another single person who would care except Hunter.

Sounds great. Now go focus so I can too.

She sends me a smiley face. It makes me smile the rest of the day. I'm falling for Kate. This time I'm going to keep falling until I see where I land.

Chapter Twenty-eight

I want you to meet my family," Kate says. It's a cold Saturday night and we're snuggled on my couch, enjoying the warmth of the fire and each other's company. We've been together officially a month now. It's been perfect.

"Okay." I'm slow to answer her and she seems concerned.

"Do you not want to?" she asks.

"Oh, I do. I just want to make sure they are okay with us. That they know we're girlfriends. Is that going to freak them out or anything?"

"They'll be fine. They're getting better with everything. Even my dad asked about you," she says. Begrudgingly, I'm sure. She threads her fingers through mine and tugs on my hand trying to get me to make a decision.

"When?" I ask. She smiles at me.

"How about next weekend? I can cook dinner at my dad's house and we can all sit down to a nice meal and good conversation." I'm skeptical only because I know her little sister still isn't completely on board about Kate being a lesbian. Teenagers aren't afraid of being vocal and, apparently, she's got a great set of lungs.

"Can I bring Maddox?"

"Of course. I was planning on you bringing him anyway. My sister is a complete dog lover and he will only help us out."

"Okay, we can do it, but at the first sign of trouble, Maddox and I are gone. I'm not going to screw your family life up. You've done so much to repair the relationship and I'll hate myself if it goes bad."

She kisses my hand softly. "It will be fine. They will love you, I promise." I'm not convinced, but I nod. There's no sense in getting upset over something that hasn't happened yet. I know her relationship with them is still tender, but getting stronger by the day.

"So let's go over everybody. I know Gary, he's nineteen and a freshman at OSU. He's on the football team and really into science and gaming. Basically, he's a typical guy. Annabeth is sixteen, popular, likes sports, plans to be a veterinarian, and hates all adults. Your father is a business man. He likes rock climbing, cooking shows, and buying his kids expensive cars." Kate tickles me until I yelp. "It's true. He got you a Mercedes, your brother got a Jeep Cherokee, and your sister is getting a Ford Escape. All great cars, all expensive."

"He's just making sure his children are safe. I got the nicer car because I'm older and I haven't been a financial burden on him for the last six years."

"My first car was a piece of shit. We called her P.I.T.A. She was always breaking down. My parents would get calls from my friends saying they saw me pushing it on this or that highway. I walked more than I drove in high school," I say.

"Why P.I.T.A.? Was she a hatchback and shaped funny?" Kate asks.

I bust out laughing. "P.I.T.A. stands for Pain In The Ass. Rightfully so, I promise. Now, I'm very sensitive about my cars and cycle them every two years. The only time I need Triple A is when Hunter and I are chasing."

Kate tells me about her first car and I sit there and just stare at her.

"Why are you smiling at me?" she asks.

"This is great. I'm getting to know you better. It's nice that you're opening up to me. This is what I was missing before with you," I say.

"New beginnings. The old me isn't around anymore." I nod my head. That Kate is gone.

"I like this Kate. I really do." Kate and I have been together every weekend for the last four weeks and we have yet to watch TV except for the Weather Channel. That's background music for us. We've worked on school work together. We've cooked meals, sanded and painted the basement, taken long drives into the country with Maddox, and worked on us as a couple. It's never boring with her. A part of me is worried that the long distance thing will weigh on us eventually. We haven't talked about what happens after she graduates. I know that she's been working on her resume. I don't know if she's going to try to get a job with OSU or what. I'm almost afraid to open that door.

"Agreed. I never knew it could be like this, you know? Not that I want to bring up other relationships, but this is my first real, mature relationship where we talk things out and do more than just…" She stops short before she incriminates herself. I lift my eyebrow at her. "Well, you know what I mean." Knowing how sexual Kate is, I can only imagine how she was with other, younger lovers. I try to not think about it. I kiss her temple instead.

"It's getting late. Let me put out this fire and let's go to bed." I'm sleepy so sex might have to wait until morning. Kate and Maddox head upstairs while I lock up and clear away our wineglasses and snacks.

Kate is in the bathroom when I head upstairs. Maddox is down on his bed, curled up, snoring softly. I head to the closet for boxers and a T-shirt and almost fall asleep putting them on. I'm crawling into bed when Kate comes out of the bathroom. She is wearing a pale blue lingerie set with strategically placed lace and sheer fabric. Suddenly sleep isn't important. I reach out, anxious to feel her soft skin under my fingertips and taste her sweetness again.

CHAPTER TWENTY-NINE

I look at the address that Kate texted me earlier and look at the house in front of me. I do that a few times before it dawns on me that I'm at the right place and this mansion in front of me is her family's house. I whistle low and Maddox perks up. Suddenly, I wish I was wearing something a little bit nicer than slacks and a scoop neck sweater. Kate and I would have driven together, but I had to stay in Norman and teach a cluster course today. The instructor has the flu and they asked me to step in. Great opportunity, crappy timing. I send Kate a text that we're here. I don't get out of the car until I see the front door open and Kate's head pop out, looking for us. I'm in disbelief that this is her place. She waves us in and Maddox and I get out of the car.

"You made it. Perfect timing." She gives me a hug and a brief kiss on the lips. I have a bottle of wine for the adults and sparkling cider for the teens. That's either going to be a hit or they are going to think I'm a total loser.

"You never told me you're rich. Like million dollar house, rich."

She looks startled and confused. "Why does it matter?"

"It doesn't, but I would have dressed nicer."

She kisses me again. "You look fantastic. Come on in and meet everybody." I make Maddox heel until the proper introductions are made. I wring my hands together until Kate reaches out and locks my fingers with hers, stopping my nervous habit. We reach the kitchen where I can see three heads watching a football game on television in the hearth room. "Tris and Maddox are here everybody." I'm greeted with relatively friendly hellos. Gary is the first to approach us.

"Tristan, it's good to see you again. Thank you for coming." He gives me a brief hug. Maybe this won't be terrible.

"It's good to see you again, Gary."

I watch Maddox walk into the hearth room and find Annabeth immediately. He nudges her and within a few moments, he has fallen in her lap and she is rubbing his chest as if they have been best friends forever.

"And that attention hog is Maddox," I say, introducing Maddox who has no interest in anybody but Annabeth.

"Kate told us about him. Come here, boy," Gary says. He pats his leg and Maddox looks at him like he's crazy. That gets Annabeth to giggle.

"Your charms aren't working on him. He wants to be with me," Annabeth says. She waves hi to me. Not super friendly, but I'll take it. Kate lifts her eyebrows at me. Apparently, that's better than she expected, too. Ben is hanging back watching us. I'm trying not to notice, but I'm keeping my distance from Kate in case I reach for her out of habit. Their relationship is too fresh for me to ruin with a simple touch. I stay focused on Maddox because it's easy and he's the tension breaker in the room.

"Once he's found his soul mate in the room, it's hard to drag him away." That makes Annabeth smile even wider. So far so good. I leave Maddox with the teens and head back into the kitchen. Kate smiles at me. She looks great and relaxed.

"Would you like a drink, Tristan?" Ben asks. He has finally found his way into the kitchen with us.

"A glass of ice water would be great." He hands me a glass and I try hard not to shake when I take it from him. I nod my thanks and he leaves the room.

"What are you cooking, Kate?" I walk over to her, happy to see her and be near her again.

"Vegetable lasagna, dinner salad, and bread. Simple, easy, good," she says. I almost kiss her, but freeze suddenly remembering that I'm in her family home and under close scrutiny. I look around, but I don't think anybody noticed.

"Sorry," I say, almost whispering.

"Don't worry about it. Everything is fine. You're in my life now and they're just going to have to accept it. I don't get upset when I see their partners fawning all over them. Well, except Annabeth's boyfriend. He's an ass," she says.

"To be expected, though," I say. She nods reluctantly. I'm glad it's just the family. I couldn't imagine a dinner party with any more people. "Is your dad seeing anyone?" I'm surprised that I don't know the answer.

"If he is, he's not sharing. I haven't seen anybody around. I know he's very busy with work." I look around the house at all of the beautiful décor and top of the line furniture. Even the silverware and cookware is stuff I've only ever dreamed of having. He must work a ton to afford all of these luxuries.

"Do you need help with anything?" I ask even though I know the answer.

"No. Just go sit with the family and get to know them. Dinner is almost ready."

I head to the hearth room and, before I get a chance to worry about where I should sit, Gary stands up and offers me his spot on the couch. He scoots over, giving me enough room.

"Best seat in the house," he says. His smile is very genuine and very much like Kate's. "Kate said you are a teacher at OU. Do you like it?"

"It's challenging. I'm just getting started there, really. I teach only one semester during the fall. I storm chase during the spring semester and I process the data during the summer. It's a full time job, but I really enjoy it."

"I'm thinking about studying Education. I'd like to teach elementary or grade school kids. And coach them. Ideally, I'd love to play for the NFL, but that probably won't happen. I love kids and I think that's something I would like to do. My dad wants me to get into business, but I just don't care for it, really."

"Teaching is rewarding, but so is business. The good news about college is that the first two years you have to take a ton of classes that might steer you one way or the other. Who knows, you might end up in the NFL. What position do you play?" I ask.

"Quarterback. Second string. I love it," he says.

"How old is Maddox?" Annabeth asks.

"He's almost three years old."

"He's such a good dog. Kate said he was hurt when he was a puppy. Where did you get him?" she asks.

"Somebody from our department heard something crying somewhere behind our building. We all spread out until we found a tiny little puppy. I fell in love with him the moment I saw him. He gave me a sad, but trusting look and I knew that I was going to protect him from that moment on no matter what."

"How did he get these scars?" she asks.

"Somebody had already hurt him by the time we found him," I say. I don't want to tell her the horrors of his history and she doesn't push.

"That's awful. He's beautiful and so sweet." She bends down and kisses his head. He responds by licking her entire face. Everybody laughs.

"Yeah, he's a total lover. He really is the best dog I've ever had," I say.

"Kate said he was great out in the field. Does he help find people after tornadoes hit?" she asks.

"Not really. I mean, he has before, but he's not trained to do so. I'm sure it's just instinct. He's very aware when there is danger and is cautious," I say.

"Are you worried that he's going to get hurt?"

"Yes. I don't let him out of the car when we're in a place where there is tornado debris because he might step on nails or sharp objects. Lesson learned." I tell her about all of the obedience classes we've taken over the years and how much time I spend with him one-on-one. She's genuinely interested and I'm happy we're talking so much. "That's the hardest part of having a pet. You need to make sure you have the time. I'm lucky because Maddox is our department mascot and they love him. I take him to work every day. He stays in my office when I have classes, but the rest of the time he is right next to me."

"I'm too busy for a dog." Annabeth sounds sad.

"Well, Maddox loves attention so whenever you feel the need, he would love a date with you," I say. Annabeth smiles at me. I'm so in with this girl. I'll have to give Maddox an extra treat tonight for knowing exactly what to do and who to charm.

"Dinner's ready," Kate says.

I'm amazed at how fast the television is shut off. Within a minute, everybody is in the kitchen helping Kate put the food on the table. My mother has to give us at least a ten minute warning if we're watching a show or a game for us to even think about heading to the dining room.

"It looks great, sis," Gary says. He and Ben are standing next to their chairs talking about the game. I notice they don't sit until we all do. Tonight is full of surprises. And here I thought chivalry was just another word in the dictionary. We pass the food around and compliment Kate on her culinary masterpiece. Our conversation is fluid and even Annabeth joins in. She's very intrigued by storm chasing. I keep the stories light and fluffy. No one wants to hear the heavy and sad. Even when Annabeth asks about Kate's accident, I keep it informative, but not descriptive.

"It was a wedge tornado. They are the fat ones that take up a lot of space and their size rapidly changes. That's what happened when the tornado hit their truck," I say.

"That must have been awful to see it happen right in front of you," Annabeth says. I don't tell her that I wanted to throw up and that I was crying and Hunter had to calm me down.

"It wasn't fun. We were lucky to be right there and able to get help immediately." Kate squeezes my knee underneath the table. We never talk about the details of that day. It was a bad time in our relationship and neither of us really want to go there. I've told Kate how scared I was, but I don't tell her how I found her all bloodied and banged up. I leave out the gory details to the family, but tell them the essentials and throw in how Maddox was concerned. That lightens the mood and it's nice to see the kids smiling.

"I'd love to go out with you guys one time," Gary says. Without even looking at him, I know Ben disapproves. I don't blame him. He almost lost one child to a tornado.

"Well, let's see what next season is like." I'm non-committal and that seems to appease both Ben and Gary.

The rest of dinner goes smoothly. The kids talk about school and work. Ben pipes up from time to time, but is relatively quiet during the meal. Kate's quiet, too, and that surprises me. Since we've reconciled, she has become a lot more talkative. It's hard to even picture her before when she kept her nose in her notebook, practically ignoring us.

"I cheated and bought dessert, guys," Kate says. "I simply ran out of time."

She jumps up and starts coffee. Gary and Annabeth clean up the plates and load the dishwasher. Ben and I are left alone and continue our conversation about The Food Network. Apparently, we share a strong love for competition cook-offs. It becomes apparent that neither one of us can cook worth a damn, but we sure have opinions about who should have their own show and who shouldn't.

"Hey, let's give it a rest you two," Kate says. She hands Ben and I coffee and Gary follows with cake. We change the topic to winter, my least favorite, yet most active season here in Oklahoma. Last year's ice storm took out two of my elm trees and a beautiful conifer I was nursing back to health after it suffered from a previous ice storm.

"Have you ever wanted to work for a news station?" Gary asks me.

"No, I like the freedom that the university affords me. I pretty much get to do what I want. I like teaching what I know and I like seeing weather unfold out in the field. I have a feeling Hunter and I are going to head south next season. Georgia, Mississippi and Alabama have been hit hard by powerful storms the last two seasons while we've stayed mainly in the Midwest." Even though I want to go on and on, I know that I have to keep their interest so I reluctantly stop. Besides, my weather phenomenon explanations have nothing to do with why I don't want to work for a news station.

"So are the people on television real meteorologists or just pretty faces the networks hire?" Annabeth asks.

"Both, I think. They know their stuff, but they rely on a team of specialists who gather the data for them. They're just the ones comfortable in front of a camera." I leave out the part that several I know are pompous jerks.

"Do you ever do interviews?" Annabeth's really interested in what I do.

"I try not to. Usually reporters want to talk to somebody right after the fact and we're either helping people or gathering data. We were in Greensburg, Kansas when the tornado struck. That's the only time I've ever willingly given an interview. That was mass destruction. Storm chasing can be exciting, but you have to learn how to handle the bad, too."

"Okay, let's talk about something else," Kate says. She sits down next to me and reaches out for my hand. This is our first official public display of affection in front of her family.

I stiffen, but nobody says anything or reacts. "Gary, when is football over?"

"We have a few more weeks." Before he can really get into the conversation, we're interrupted by Gary's phone.

"Well, that's Kayla. I need to get going." He stands and reaches over to shake my hand. "Tristan, it's good to see you again and meet your dog who ignored me the whole night." We all laugh. He waves to all of us and quickly leaves. Ben looks at Annabeth.

"Is Rob coming over tonight?" he asks.

"No, Kate said tonight was family night," she says. I can see her face fall, crushed that her older brother got to go out, but not her.

"I didn't mean that you couldn't go out. I just wanted you here for dinner with us," Kate says. Annabeth rolls her eyes.

"Well, you could have told me that sooner," she says. She picks up her phone and heads for the stairs. She looks back at me. "Thanks for coming, Tristan. Maddox is cool." She disappears before I can respond. Ben and Kate chuckle.

"That went way better than expected," Kate says. Ben nods in agreement.

"If you don't mind, I'm headed to my office. If you need me, just holler," Ben says. He grabs his coffee and leaves. Kate and I are finally alone.

"What did you think?" I ask.

"What did you think?" she asks.

"I think it went okay. I'm still scared of your dad though. The only time he really talked to me was when we talked about all the different cooking shows."

She smiles. "We all fear Big Ben. I'm surprised at Annabeth. I knew Gary would be charming. Annabeth was respectful. Thank God Maddox was here." She reaches down and pets him.

"Yeah, it looks like you've got competition for Maddox's attention."

"Well, as long as I don't have any competition for yours, I'm fine," she says. I quickly kiss her.

"How long are we staying?" I can't wait to touch her. I haven't seen her in six days.

"We can leave now. Let's go tell my dad." She grabs my hand and we walk down the long hallway until we reach Ben's office. Even though the door is ajar, Kate knocks. "Dad? We are getting ready to leave. We came to say bye."

"Come on in," he says. His office is massive and full of dark cherry furniture. I'm instantly in love with it.

"What a beautiful office," I say.

"Thank you." He walks over to us and reaches out for my hand. "It was good to see you again, Tristan. This time under better circumstances." I nod in agreement. "Have a nice evening." He leans over and kisses Kate on her cheek. As we turn to leave his office, my eyes catch a stack of papers on his desk because I see the words University of Oklahoma. Something inside clicks. I stop. Kate looks at me puzzled.

"Are you okay?" she asks.

"Can you give me a quick moment with your father?" I ask. She's surprised, but covers it well and nods.

"Sure. I'll let Maddox out before we head to my place." She leaves and closes the door. I'm glad she didn't push me for a reason. I'm sure that will come later.

"Ben, can I ask you something?" I ask. He motions for me to sit down in the wingback chair to the side of his desk. I sit down slowly, my mind going a million miles a minute trying to figure out how to ask the question. "Our school received an anonymous donation last month. A very generous one. We don't know who it's from, but my name is the only staff member's on the paperwork. I just want to know if you know anything about that?" He stares at me forever, his blue eyes piercing mine. I'm trying hard not to look away. "I don't know anybody who could give that kind of money and most people want the world to know when they've contributed to support a university or a cause."

"Well, I think that anonymous means the contributor doesn't want people to know he or she has made the contribution. Perhaps there's a good reason." The more I think about it, the more I'm certain it's him. I don't know anybody else who has that kind of money. Plus, I'm sure Kate did a guilt trip number on him this summer when she found out he was behind her landing the government grant.

"Perhaps his daughter attends a rival school and if word got out that he contributed to it, people might get the wrong impression." It's a bold move, but I throw it out there to see if he'll take the bait.

"It's entirely possible. Hypothetically speaking, maybe he did the wrong thing previously and this is a way to make things right." I don't know how to react now. Obviously, he wants to keep it under wraps, but how do I thank him? I can't just pretend he didn't save my ass or several jobs with this generous endowment.

"Well, let me state that our department is completely in this person's debt and I'm eternally grateful for his generosity," I say. He actually winks at me. We leave it at that. He walks me to the office door. "Have a good rest of your weekend with Kate." I practically skip down the hall. Kate rounds the corner with Maddox and I almost bump into them.

"You ready?" she asks. I nod. It's hard not to smile.

"What?" she asks.

"We'll talk about it later. Let's get back to your place." Maddox follows us out. As nice as this place is, I really just want to be alone with Kate in her cute little apartment celebrating us. It's been almost a week since I felt her warm body against mine.

CHAPTER THIRTY

Okay, you know I'm not one to pump you for information and stuff, right?" Kate asks. I nod. It's two in the morning and I'm in the aftermath of really good sex and the soft space right before I fall asleep. "And I never ask you what you're doing or who you're with, right?" I think I nod. "So are you going to tell me what you and my father were talking about?" That wakes me up. She's put me in a bad spot. I don't want to lie to her, but I don't want to reveal Ben's actions. He wants to keep it anonymous. Obviously, my relationship with Kate is far more important, but this could have a snowball effect. She will either love her father even more, or get pissed that he's gotten involved again.

"I was talking to him about the donation our department received, that's all. Remember that anonymous cashier's check we got? Well, I was asking your father if he knew anything about it."

"What did he say?"

"He didn't confess." Technically this is true. "But I got the impression that it was him."

"I wouldn't put it past him. He was clearly upset after I explained the consequences of his actions," she says. I relax. She's not mad. I put my arms around her and pull her close to me.

"It's late. Let's go to sleep, love," I say. I can feel her smile against me.

"You just called me love," she says. And I'm fully awake again. Did I really? I try not to tense up as I allow my fuzzy brain to recall the last ten seconds. Yep, I did. Well, that was a slip. It's either time to spill my true feelings or pretend to be asleep. The latter sounds less complicated, but telling her how I really feel sounds wonderful.

"Yes, I did," I say. We're both very quiet for a few moments.

"Why?" she asks. This really isn't the way I want this particular conversation to go down. I want to be in front of the fireplace at my house, drinking wine and listening to soft jazz, not naked and freezing in her tiny apartment at two in the morning, tired, after a stressful night of meeting her family.

"I don't suppose you'll wait until morning to let me answer that?" I ask. She pinches me. "Ow! Okay, okay. I said that because I mean it. You're my love." I sit up and untangle us so that we're looking at one another. "I love you, Kate. I really do." She's not smiling and for a split second, I panic. Tears well up in her eyes and my eyes widen with fear. "Don't cry, love." I say it again. That makes the tears fall. I cup her face in my hands and make her look at me. "Is that not okay with you?" Now her bottom lip quivers. I have no idea what's going on right now. She reaches out for me and I hold her close. Now she's actually sobbing. Christ. This isn't going the way I had planned at all. Even Maddox looks over at us. "Kate, Kate, it's okay," I say. I run my hand up and down her back, trying everything I can to make her stop crying.

"No, it's good. It's really good. I'm happy." She looks up at me. I wipe her tears away and smile at her.

"You aren't supposed to cry like this when you're happy." I smile to let her know I'm kidding. I breathe a sigh of relief. She laughs a bit. It sounds garbled and emotional, but better than her sobs. I kiss her forehead again and pull her close to me again to hold her.

"Tristan, I love you, too. I have for a long time. Probably since your birthday," she says.

"Really?" I ask. Suddenly, I'm no longer tired.

"I know I haven't been easy and we have a lot in our past, but I do love you and I really want us to work." She's finally calm enough to look at me. "I'm not going to screw up again. I might make you angry from time to time, but that's not my intent." She places her hand over my heart. "This is the best present in the world. Your heart." Great. Now, my eyes fill with tears.

"I know we're going to make it work. There's nobody else in the world I can imagine myself with. You're absolutely perfect for me. For us," I say, nodding at Maddox. He's been right by the bed since he heard Kate cry. She reaches out and pets him quickly to let him know she's fine. Satisfied, he goes back to the bed Kate made him out of a quilt.

"Since you came into my life, I've found my family and my heart again. The last six years have been so empty and I've been so alone. I can never thank you enough for giving it all back to me." She snuggles against me again. The adrenaline rush of our confession has given me new life and I have a better idea that doesn't involve sleeping. I lean up on my elbow so that I'm looking directly at her.

"I don't give my heart easily. I trust you and I love you. We'll make this work. I can't imagine my life without you. I look forward to our visits, our phone calls, holding you, making love to you, kissing you, sharing with you." I lean down and kiss her softly. This is our first kiss after confessing our love and I can already tell it's different. She moves her body closer to me and I deepen the kiss. Her moan encourages me to continue and I slip a leg between hers. She wraps her arms around my waist, holding me closer. I break the kiss to trail my lips down her neck, savoring the sweet, smooth taste of her skin against my tongue. I touch her collarbone with my fingertips and smile when I feel her nails in the back of my neck, scratching softly through my hair.

"You're beautiful and all mine," I say. I cup her breast and gently lick her nipple, feasting on the sensitive bud until I feel her squirm beneath me. I give the same amount of attention to her other nipple while I slowly slip my entire body between her legs. I feel her hips raise slightly at my weight, her need for friction building. I'm surprised she isn't sensitive since we both just had amazing orgasms less than half an hour ago. I reach between her legs and am surprised at how wet she is for me. I slowly run my fingers up and down her slit until I hear her hiss through clenched teeth.

"Tristan." Her voice is low and shaky. It's perfect. Her voice sounds exactly like the way I'm feeling. Emotional, heartfelt, and raw. I slip inside of her, marveling at her wet warmth and how she molds around me, her tightness clutching my fingers. I move slowly, gently at first until I know she is ready for more. It doesn't take long for her hips to move against my hand so I speed up and work my mouth down her smooth, soft stomach. I can feel her quivering against my lips, taste the thin layer of sweat as her body works with mine to reach bliss again. Her moans are music to my ears. I've never wanted to please another woman more. It isn't long before I'm at the junction of her thighs where I begin a slow seduction with my tongue. Her clit is hard and I can feel her heartbeat. She isn't going to last much longer. My fingers are steadily building her up, while my mouth gives her the friction she needs. Again, her hands find the back of my neck, but this time she is clutching my hair, allowing me to do whatever I want to her. This is the new Kate. This is her giving herself to me fully. We have trust tonight and from this night forward. Her hips start moving in tiny circles and I know she is ready. I give her what her body is asking for. She cries out at her release and reaches for me the moment she has strength again. I crawl up next to her and hold her as tears stream down her face. This is her happy cry.

"You're incredible. I'm never letting you go." She holds me close to her and for the first time in our relationship, I really believe her. My heart knows it and my soul feels it. Kate is everything to me. My happiness, my determination, my true better half. This whirlwind romance that took us both by surprise has turned into the best decision of my life and my heart.

Epilogue

Hunter hates me, doesn't she?" Kate asks. I'm helping her with her necklace as she completes her outfit for her first day of work at Channel 4 in Oklahoma City. I give her a quick kiss on her neck to let her know I'm done. She turns to me. "I'm going to do a good job. I'll show her it's not that bad." I kiss her softly.

"Don't worry about Hunter. She's probably jealous. You're going to do a fantastic job. You're smart, you know your weather, and they are lucky to have you."

Kate moved in with me last month. There was no reason for her to stay in Stillwater after her graduation, so I asked her to move to Norman. Maddox and I love having her here. I'm excited to go home and sometimes Maddox stays with her during the day. That will change now that she accepted the job at KFOR for their weather team. She will be working the equipment behind the scenes, but Hunter and I have a bet going on when they'll put her in front of the camera. I say two years. Hunter thinks it will be sooner than that.

"It is kind of exciting. I'll actually get paid to do what I was doing at the university." Kate is still very determined to make it on her own even though her relationship with her father has only improved over the last few months. She won't touch her trust fund or accept anything from her father other than his love. Her car was considered a trade. I've never seen a Honda nice enough to rival a Mercedes, but I'm not going to argue her logic. I'm just happy she's safe. I hand her a mug of hot coffee and her bag.

"You don't want to be late on your first day, love," I say. She smiles at me.

"Can you believe I got up so early?"

"Today will probably be the one and only day you do."

She laughs and slips inside her car. "Have a good day. Take care of my guy for me." It's amazing how fast Maddox attached himself to Kate. Today will be a sad day for him, but he'll be fine. I'll let him wander a bit around the department instead of keeping him in my office all day.

"Be safe and let me know how you're doing." Maddox and I stand in the driveway until she pulls out onto the highway. I can't believe my life has changed so fast, so beautifully in just a short time. I met Kate just nine months ago and even though I never thought in a million years I'd be sharing my life with her, we wake up together every day, go to bed every night and share our thoughts, our desires, and our love. It's a fairy tale life, but I think we both deserve this happy ending.

About the Author

Kris Bryant grew up a military brat living in several different countries before her family settled down in the Midwest when she was twelve. Books were her only form of entertainment overseas, and she read anything and everything within her reach. Reading eventually turned into writing when she decided she didn't like the way some of the novels ended and wanted to give the characters she fell in love with the ending she thought they so deserved. Earning a B.A. in English from the University of Missouri, Kris focused more on poetry, and after some encouragement from her girlfriend, decided to tackle her own book. In her spare time, Kris enjoys traveling, hiking, photography, spending time with her Westie pup, Molly, and hanging out with her family.

Kris's debut novel, *Jolt*, was a Lambda Literary Finalist for Lesbian Romance.

Books Available from Bold Strokes Books

Love on Tap by Karis Walsh. Beer and romance are brewing for Tace Lomond when archaeologist Berit Katsaros comes into her life. (987-1-162639-564-0)

Love on the Red Rocks by Lisa Moreau. An unexpected romance at a lesbian resort forces Malley to face her greatest fears where she must choose between playing it safe or taking a chance at true happiness. (987-1-162639-660-9)

Tracker and the Spy by D. Jackson Leigh. There are lessons for all when Captain Tanisha is assigned untried pyro Kyle and a lovesick dragon horse for a mission to track the leader of a dangerous cult. (987-1-162639-448-3)

Whirlwind Romance by Kris Bryant. Will chasing the girl break Tristan's heart or give her something she's never had before? (987-1-162639-581-7)

Whiskey Sunrise by Missouri Vaun. Culture and religion collide when Lovey Porter, daughter of a local Baptist minister, falls for the handsome thrill-seeking moonshine runner, Royal Duval. (987-1-162639-519-0)

Dyre: By Moon's Light by Rachel E. Bailey. A young werewolf, Des, guards the aging leader of all the Packs: the Dyre. Stable employment—nice work, if you can get it…at least until silver bullets start to fly. (978-1-62639-6-623)

Fragile Wings by Rebecca S. Buck. In Roaring Twenties London, can Evelyn Hopkins find love with Jos Singleton or will the scars of the Great War crush her dreams? (978-1-62639-5-466)

Live and Love Again by Jan Gayle. Jessica Whitney could be Sarah Jarret's second chance at love, but their differences and Sarah's grief continue to come between their budding relationship. (978-1-62639-5-176)

Starstruck by Lesley Davis. Actress Cassidy Hayes and writer Aiden Darrow find out the hard way not all life-threatening drama is confined to the TV screen or the pages of a manuscript. (978-1-62639-5-237)

Stealing Sunshine by Tina Michele. Under the Central Florida sun, two women struggle between fear and love as a dangerous plot of deception and revenge threatens to steal priceless art and lives. (978-1-62639-4-452)

The Fifth Gospel by Michelle Grubb. Hiding a Vatican secret is dangerous—sharing the secret suicidal—can Felicity survive a perilous book tour, and will her PR specialist, Anna, be there when it's all over? (978-1-62639-4-476)

Cold to the Touch by Cari Hunter. A drug addict's murder is the start of a dangerous investigation for Detective Sanne Jensen and Dr. Meg Fielding, as they try to stop a killer with no conscience. (978-1-62639-526-8)

Forsaken by Laydin Michaels. The hunt for a killer teaches one woman that she must overcome her fear in order to love, and another that success is meaningless without happiness. (978-1-62639-481-0)

Infiltration by Jackie D. When a CIA breach is imminent, a Marine instructor must stop the attack while protecting her heart from being disarmed by a recruit. (978-1-62639-521-3)

Midnight at the Orpheus by Alyssa Linn Palmer. Two women desperate to make their way in the world, a man hell-bent on revenge, and a cop risking his career: all in a day's work in Capone's Chicago. (978-1-62639-607-4)

Spirit of the Dance by Mardi Alexander. Major Sorla Reardon's return to her family farm to heal threatens Riley Johnson's safe life when small-town secrets are revealed, and love may not conquer all. (978-1-62639-583-1)

Sweet Hearts by Melissa Brayden, Rachel Spangler, and Karis Walsh. Do you ever wonder *Whatever happened to*...? Find out when you reconnect with your favorite characters from Melissa Brayden's *Heart Block*, Rachel Spangler's *LoveLife*, and Karis Walsh's *Worth the Risk*. (978-1-62639-475-9)

Totally Worth It by Maggie Cummings. Who knew there's an all-lesbian condo community in the NYC suburbs? Join twentysomething BFFs Meg and Lexi at Bay West as they navigate friendships, love, and everything in between. (978-1-62639-512-1)

Illicit Artifacts by Stevie Mikayne. Her foster mother's death cracked open a secret world Jil never wanted to see…and now she has to pick up the stolen pieces. (978-1-62639-472-8)

Pathfinder by Gun Brooke. Heading for their new homeworld, Exodus's chief engineer Adina Vantressa and nurse Briar Lindemay carry game-changing secrets that may well cause them to lose everything when disaster strikes. (978-1-62639-444-5)

Prescription for Love by Radclyffe. Dr. Flannery Rivers finds herself attracted to the new ER chief, city girl Abigail Remy, and the incendiary mix of city and country, fire and ice, tradition and change is combustible. (978-1-62639-570-1)

Ready or Not by Melissa Brayden. Uptight Mallory Spencer finds relinquishing control to bartender Hope Sanders too tall an order in fast-paced New York City. (978-1-62639-443-8)

Summer Passion by MJ Williamz. Women loving women is forbidden in 1946 Hollywood, yet Jean and Maggie strive to keep their love alive and away from prying eyes. (978-1-62639-540-4)

The Princess and the Prix by Nell Stark. "Ugly duckling" Princess Alix of Monaco was resigned to loneliness until she met racecar driver Thalia d'Angelis. (978-1-62639-474-2)

Winter's Harbor by Aurora Rey. Lia Brooks isn't looking for love in Provincetown, but when she discovers chocolate croissants and pastry chef Alex McKinnon, her winter retreat quickly starts heating up. (978-1-62639-498-8)

The Time Before Now by Missouri Vaun. Vivian flees a disastrous affair, embarking on an epic, transformative journey to escape her past, until destiny introduces her to Ida, who helps her rediscover trust, love, and hope. (978-1-62639-446-9)

Twisted Whispers by Sheri Lewis Wohl. Betrayal, lies, and secrets—whispers of a friend lost to darkness. Can a reluctant psychic set things right or will an evil soul destroy those she loves? (978-1-62639-439-1)

The Courage to Try by C.A. Popovich. Finding love is worth getting past the fear of trying. (978-1-62639-528-2)

Break Point by Yolanda Wallace. In a world readying for war, can love find a way? (978-1-62639-568-8)

Countdown by Julie Cannon. Can two strong-willed, powerful women overcome their differences to save the lives of seven others and begin a life they never imagined together? (978-1-62639-471-1)

Keep Hold by Michelle Grubb. Claire knew some things should be left alone and some rules should never be broken, but the most forbidden, well, they are the most tempting. (978-1-62639-502-2)

Deadly Medicine by Jaime Maddox. Dr. Ward Thrasher's life is in turmoil. Her partner Jess left her, and her job puts her in the path of a murderous physician who has Jess in his sights. (978-1-62639-424-7)

New Beginnings by KC Richardson. Can the connection and attraction between Jordan Roberts and Kirsten Murphy be enough for Jordan to trust Kirsten with her heart? (978-1-62639-450-6)

Officer Down by Erin Dutton. Can two women who've made careers out of being there for others in crisis find the strength to need each other? (978-1-62639-423-0)

Reasonable Doubt by Carsen Taite. Just when Sarah and Ellery think they've left dangerous careers behind, a new case sets them—and their hearts—on a collision course. (978-1-62639-442-1)

Tarnished Gold by Ann Aptaker. Cantor Gold must outsmart the Law, outrun New York's dockside gangsters, outplay a shady art dealer, his lover, and a beautiful curator, and stay out of a killer's gun sights. (978-1-62639-426-1)

White Horse in Winter by Franci McMahon. Love between two women collides with the inner poison of a closeted horse trainer in the green hills of Vermont. (978-1-62639-429-2)

Autumn Spring by Shelley Thrasher. Can Bree and Linda, two women in the autumn of their lives, put their hearts first and find the love they've never dared seize? (978-1-62639-365-3)

The Renegade by Amy Dunne. Post-apocalyptic survivors Alex and Evelyn secretly find love while held captive by a deranged cult, but when their relationship is discovered, they must fight for their freedom—or die trying. (978-1-62639-427-8)

Thrall by Barbara Ann Wright. Four women in a warrior society must work together to lift an insidious curse while caught between their own desires, the will of their peoples, and an ancient evil. (978-1-62639-437-7)

The Chameleon's Tale by Andrea Bramhall. Two old friends must work through a web of lies and deceit to find themselves again, but in the search they discover far more than they ever went looking for. (978-1-62639-363-9)